WE DIDN'T THINK
IT THROUGH

T0347203

Also by Gary Lonesborough

The Boy from the Mish

WE DIDN'T THINK IT THROUGH

GARY LONESBOROUGH

ALLEN&UNWIN
SYDNEY • MELBOURNE • AUCKLAND • LONDON

First published by Allen & Unwin in 2023

Copyright © text, Gary Lonesborough 2023
Copyright © cover art, Hafleg (Shaun Lee) 2023

All rights reserved. No part of this book may be reproduced or transmitted in
any form or by any means, electronic or mechanical, including photocopying,
recording or by any information storage and retrieval system, without prior
permission in writing from the publisher. The Australian *Copyright Act 1968*
(the Act) allows a maximum of one chapter or 10 per cent of this book, whichever
is the greater, to be photocopied by any educational institution for its educational
purposes provided that the educational institution (or body that administers it) has
given a remuneration notice to the Copyright Agency (Australia) under the Act.

Allen & Unwin
Cammeraygal Country
83 Alexander Street
Crows Nest NSW 2065
Australia
Phone: (61 2) 8425 0100
Email: info@allenandunwin.com
Web: www.allenandunwin.com

*Allen & Unwin acknowledges the Traditional Owners of the Country on which we
live and work. We pay our respects to all Aboriginal and Torres Strait Islander
Elders, past and present.*

A catalogue record for this
book is available from the
National Library of Australia

ISBN 978 1 76052 693 1

For teaching resources, explore www.allenandunwin.com/resources/for-teachers

Cover and text design by Kirby Armstrong and Sandra Nobes
Set in 11.5/16.5 pt Adobe Garamond Pro by Midland Typesetters, Australia
Printed and bound in Australia by the Opus Group

10 9 8 7 6 5 4 3 2 1

The paper in this book is FSC® certified.
FSC® promotes environmentally responsible,
socially beneficial and economically viable
management of the world's forests.

www.garylonesborough.com

For Mum and Dad,
and all young First Nations people like Jamie,
whose stories are never heard

PART 1
THE BOY

1

The Aboriginal youth worker is rambling on about *cultural initiations* and *manhood*, but I'm too busy scratching the mozzie bites on my legs to pay attention. It's the last night at camp and all of us Koori kids are sitting on logs around the firepit. I'm between my best mates, Dally and Lenny.

'Reckon anyone's been murdered out here?' Dally whispers to me. He's been letting his mo grow out and he's got a weird little beard on the end of his chin, too. Well, *he* would call it a beard, but it's more like ten strands of hair clumped closely together. We had haircuts the other day and I got a trim, but he shaved to a number two.

'What you on about?'

'I mean, we're in the middle of nowhere,' Dally says. 'You can't hear no traffic from here and no one would hear you scream. I reckon this would be the perfect place to murder somebody.'

The skin on my legs is beginning to sting and there's blood on the tips of my fingers. I knew I should've put on my trackies tonight, but for some reason I thought mozzies only attacked in summer and I'd be safe because it's freezing August right now. Dark trees stand tall around us in our clearing. We're right out bush and it's just us, campfire and random noises from the dark. The noises are probably birds or insects, but it makes me wonder if there are some unknown creatures hidden in the black, watching us.

'The most important thing for you fullas to take from these camps are your goals. Let's go round the circle and say what our goal is before the end of the year,' the Aboriginal youth worker, Travis, says. Travis has dreadlocks that are tied up in a black beehive on his head. 'I'll start. My goal is to run another one of these camps with you fullas.'

Travis passes his talking stick – which isn't even like a special stick with Aboriginal art or carvings, just a stick he picked up off the ground – to the lad sitting next to him. When the lad finishes saying his goal, he passes it on to the next person.

I'm trying to think of a goal for myself. I can't concentrate, though, because my leg is too itchy and now there's blood all over the place from the mozzie bites. The stick arrives at Dally beside me.

'Umm,' Dally says. 'I guess my goal is to finish the first year of my apprenticeship.'

'Great goal,' Travis says, as Dally passes the talking stick to me.

'Uhh,' I begin, then stop to clear my throat. 'Umm... I dunno...Maybe...My voice is shaky. I swear my arms and legs are shaking, too.

4

I guess my goal should be to be better to my Aunty Dawn. I'm dreading going back home tomorrow after camp. Our blow-up on Monday night is so fresh in my mind. She opened my bedroom door, stood at my doorway with a red face and a vein popping out of her forehead, holding a scrunched packet of smokes in her hand.

'So, this morning I was putting your clothes in the wash,' Aunty Dawn said, 'and this fell out of one of your pockets.'

My stomach dropped into a black hole.

'They're not mine,' I said. 'They're Dally's. He left 'em at the youth centre yesterday. I was gonna give 'em back to him at camp.'

Aunty Dawn didn't believe me, and of course they were my smokes, but I was right in the shit and lying usually makes *the shit* go away.

'You're really pushing me lately, Jamie,' she said. 'Going out all night, coming home late, smellin' like grog. And now cigarettes? Really? I'm this close to sending you to live with your brother. You're grounded indefinitely.' I followed her into the kitchen and watched her drown the ciggies in the sink.

Before I stormed back to my bedroom, I swore at her, called her names. I didn't mean to explode, but it was like I blinked, then my head was on fire and I was yelling at her. I should have apologised before I left for camp, but I didn't. The anger, the heat, sometimes it comes so easily to me. Maybe I'm meant to be this angry person for the rest of my life. Maybe that's my thing: I'm Jamie, the *angry guy*. I don't like it, though. I wish I wasn't so short-fused sometimes. My goal should be to be better to my aunty because Aunty Dawn deserves better. She deserves so much better than me, but I can't say that to Travis or the boys.

'Uhh...My goal is...to...not die this year.'

'Right.' Travis chuckles and a few kids chuckle along with him. 'That's as good a goal as any.'

I hand the talking stick to Lenny. He's taller than me and Dally, and he's the skinniest of all us boys. Once his growth spurt hit him, we started calling him Slenderman. He hated that, of course, because he hates scary things. Lenny gets way more nervous than me in these kinds of situations. He's reserved and speaks softly. I expect Travis will ask him to repeat whatever he says, because that always happens.

'Umm,' Lenny begins, and his voice is quiet as expected. 'Well...I'm moving to Sydney next week, which is shit. So...I don't know...I don't have any goals.'

'Sure you do,' Travis says. 'Just think of anything you'd like to achieve this year. Even if it's just a small thing, it's still a goal you can set for yourself.'

'Umm, okay. Well...err...when I move to Sydney... umm...my goal...my goal this year is...to...have... a threesome.'

Everyone in the group cracks up, me included. My eyes are watering as Dally leans against me, laughing hysterically. I'm shocked, because Lenny is usually this shy lad who only really talks to me and Dally. He never says things like that to us, let alone the whole of Travis's youth camp.

But Lenny's laughing too and across the fire, Travis is blushing and shaking his head.

'Wonderful,' Travis says with a sigh. 'That's great.'

Lenny passes on the talking stick and my stomach is sore from the laughter.

'Where'd that come from?' I whisper to Lenny, quickly covering my mouth with my hand to stop myself cracking up again.

'I don't know,' Lenny whispers back. 'I'm moving, so no point in making goals. I ain't in control of anything.'

The talking stick makes its way to the last boy in the group. After he finishes telling everyone his stupid goal, Travis and Will, the other youth worker, stand.

'All right, fullas,' Travis says. 'We'll get to cooking dinner and then you have an hour of free time before bed. Before we leave the circle, I just wanna say I'm real proud-uh-you boys. Tonight's our last night, but I don't want it to end. I really enjoyed this camp, and you should all be proud of yourselves for coming along and for participating.' Travis looks at me. 'I know this was a big step out of comfort zones for some of you, and I hope you'll continue to push those boundaries and grow.'

Some of the boys get up from the logs and some head to their tents, some go for the water container.

Smoke from the barbecue fills the air of the clearing as Travis cooks some freshly caught fish and abalone, while Will deep-fries chips over the fire.

I'm first to take a plate. Using tongs, I break some fish away and drop it onto my plate, then cover it with chips. I take a piece of quartered lemon and squeeze it over the food, then use my fingers to shove some fish into my mouth.

Dally and Lenny get their own plates and sit with me on the log and eat. I pull the fishbones from my mouth as I go, then I'm onto the abalone. As soon as I take a bite, it feels like it was meant to be – like every moment in my life has been leading me to eat this abalone.

'Abs are fucking amazing,' I say to Dally. 'I've decided it's my favourite seafood.'

'It looks like a vagina,' Dally says. 'Okay, here we go.' He tastes it, gingerly at first, then he hacks into it like a frenzied shark.

When we finish, we have free time before bed. Some people go to piss behind the trees, but me, Dally and Lenny start for the toilets away from camp. Dally looks back as we begin the long walk along the dirt road downhill through the bush.

'Quick, before Andy sees us,' Dally says. Andy's my tent-mate and he's kind of part of our group, but he's a fucking motormouth who says the stupidest shit sometimes. Now that Lenny's moving, and Dally's doing his apprenticeship, Andy will be my only friend at school.

We walk a little faster and Dally uses his torch to guide our way.

'You got some balls, Len,' Dally says to Lenny. 'Where's that sense of humour been all these years?'

'Didn't want to waste it on you and Jamie,' Lenny says and it cracks me and Dally up.

It's pitch-black tonight and it's cloudy, so there aren't any stars to look at. The night-birds are whistling to each other somewhere nearby, probably trying to figure out what this crunchy, scraping noise is, but they'll never realise it's just our shoes against the gravel. Aside from our shoes on the gravel and the whistling birds, the only other sounds in my ears are the crashing waves at the beach, which grow louder the further we walk down the track. The bush seems to act like a blanket around the campgrounds, because I can't hear the boys at the clearing anymore – their chatter and laughter is hidden by the bush.

I pull my hood over my head as we arrive at the car park with the two pit toilets.

'I'm fuckin' busting,' Dally says as he races for one of the toilets, taking the torch with him. Lenny walks quickly behind him and takes the other toilet.

The clouds aren't as thick over the ocean, and moonlight is breaking through to shine over the water. I walk along the gravel and onto the grass, stopping at the top of the walkway down to the beach. I take my piss right there, looking out over the waves, which are big and foamy and crashing. The cold wind is strong as it blows over me from the beach. I'm freezing. I don't even hear my piss hitting the sand, because the waves are crashing so loud and the wind is howling against my ears. A smile comes over my face and a thought enters my mind: peace is gazing out at the waves lit by moonlight on a secluded beach while pissing on the sand.

A screech from hell rings out behind me. It zaps my whole body and a push on my back shoves me forward. I stop peeing and almost fall over, but I somehow manage to keep my footing. When I turn around, Dally's standing there, holding his stomach as he laughs his head off.

'You prick.'

The torch comes on and I follow Dally back to the car park. All the while he's still giggling to himself like he's just done the funniest thing ever. Lenny's waiting by the toilets with his hands in his pockets.

'Sorry, Jamie. I told him not to,' Lenny says.

'Fuck off.' Dally laughs. 'It was Lenny's idea!'

Back at camp, Travis and Will are both sitting by the fire with some of the boys, tuning the strings of their guitars. They begin to strum the guitars, complementing one another in this weirdly beautiful melody. It's relaxing, soothing. Then, Travis starts to sing 'Knockin' on Heaven's Door' and he's completely butchering it, like a drunk guy trying to sing like Axl Rose or something.

When they finish the song, they begin to play another and Dally and Lenny head to their tent. I go to mine where Andy's waiting inside, his face lit by the glow of his phone screen. Andy's got his red hoodie on with the hood tight around his head. He turns his phone off when I step in, shuffles into his sleeping bag and rests his head back on the pillow. Andy's got really bushy, curly hair that looks funny on the top of his skinny body. He's shorter than me and everyone else our age. He was born with foetal alcohol syndrome or disorder or something. I didn't know what that was until he told me and I looked it up.

'Bruh, my back's killing me from this shitty air mattress,' Andy says as I take off my shoes. I zip up the tent door. 'It's child abuse that we have to sleep on these. We need bigger tents, too, because you sleep with your mouth open and your breath ain't that fresh during the night, you know?'

In my head, I remind myself that he's my *friend* – he's part of my group and he's not someone I should backhand.

'I like coming out bush with you brothers, though,' Andy continues. I roll my eyes and sigh as I manoeuvre into my sleeping bag and rest my head on my icy pillow. 'I'm glad you and Lenny and Dal came along this time. Youse know what ya been missin' out on now, hey? It's like a refresher for the soul. I love it.'

I want to tell him to shut his food-hole so I can get a decent sleep. I want to tell him he should have his tongue removed or join one of those places where monks take vows of silence. But I just close my eyes, roll onto my side and face away from him.

'Night, lad.'

'Goodnight,' Andy says.

My eyes aren't even closed for five minutes before Andy starts snoring. I'm tempted to gently drag him outside and have the tent to myself tonight. My legs are starting to itch again from those friggin' mozzie bites.

I'm dreading going back home and facing Aunty Dawn. I imagine her waiting out the front of her house with all my stuff packed in bags and a one-way ticket to Sydney. I close my eyes and think about the beach, the crashing waves and the moonlight dancing over the water, the wind blowing through me.

2

The morning light is bright against the red walls of the tent. Andy's already out of his sleeping bag and I can hear Travis barking orders outside. I yawn and climb out to see most tents have been packed down already. Still half asleep, I head for Dally, who's pouring himself a cup of orange juice.

'Jamie,' Travis says, appearing from pretty much nowhere beside me, carrying a tent. 'Could you fold a couple of the chairs and bring them over to the bus?'

'I just woke up,' I say.

'It's no trouble, mate,' Travis says. 'Just grab those two there.'

'Let me just get some juice first.'

'I need you to chip in. Everyone's gotta help.'

'Just fuck off, all right? I only just fucking woke up. Give me a fucking minute.'

'Whoa,' Travis says. He stands there with his mouth wide open for a moment, then he walks away. He doesn't bother arguing with me, and now I feel shitty. I'm an arsehole. But I didn't mean to be – not really. I sigh and divert to the camping chairs behind the logs around the firepit. I pack three down and carry them to the back of the bus, load them on top of the others.

We're out of the campsite in a hurry and headed home on the bus. Travis doesn't look at me. I should say sorry when I get the chance, when he's alone and no one else can hear. We stop on the highway along the coast. Our group fills the whole inside of Maccas as we eat breakfast.

'This is the most scenic Maccas ever,' Dally says, and he's right, because out the window, you can see the beach beyond the grass. I sit with Dally, Lenny and Andy. Andy keeps talking all the way through his bacon and egg McMuffin, spitting out little pieces of egg as he speaks. Seeing the gooey pieces of white hit the table while other bits stick to his lips really kills my appetite, so I look out the window to the beach. The waves crash to the shore and reach as far up the beach as they can.

After we leave Maccas, it's an hour and a half's drive back to Dalton's Bay. The bus stops at the youth centre just after one o'clock and I see Uncle Bobby's parked across the road in his ute to pick me up.

'You sure you're not coming to the footy tonight?' Dally asks me.

'Yeah. Aunt's got the leash on me.'

'Can you ask her? It's Lenny's last Friday night with us,' Dally says.

'I don't know. Maybe. I'll text youse.'

'Okay, sweet,' Dally says.

'I'll see you before you leave,' I say to Lenny. He nods back to me.

'Catch ya,' Dally says. He and Lenny walk towards the shopping centre while I head over to Travis.

'Thanks for camp. It was fun,' I say.

'No worries, brother. Thanks for coming along,' Travis says.

I want to open my mouth again and apologise to him. It's the perfect opportunity, because Dally and Lenny have walked away and the other lingering boys are chatting among themselves. No one is within earshot. I want to apologise, and I should, but my lips won't part. I give Travis a nod and head across the road. I throw my bag onto the back tray of Uncle Bobby's ute and get in.

'How was camp?' he asks. Even though Uncle Bobby is in his sixties, he's got a beautiful full mane of silver hair.

'It was good,' I say.

'I'm glad you went along. It's great you young mob can get out bush and be among nature.'

'Yeah,' I say, as Uncle Bobby starts our drive home, out of the main street and then over the big hill towards the Valley. We drive through the neighbourhoods of the Valley and into the bush on the far side. We're not far into the bush before we come to Aunty Dawn's house.

Here we go. I take a deep breath before I follow Uncle Bobby inside. Archie Roach is playing quietly from the stereo. Aunty Dawn's on the phone with her headset on. She gives me a short glance as I pass.

'Jamie,' she says, covering her microphone. 'Run out back and get the clothes off the line for me, hey? Looks like it might storm later.'

It's not gonna storm. The anger is bubbling because I just want to get my phone on the charger and check my socials, but I should be good.

I head to my room, drop my bag to the floor and go to the laundry. I grab Aunty Dawn's big red basket and head out to the backyard. The grass is getting a bit long and Uncle Bobby's getting a bit old, so I'm beginning to worry Aunty Dawn will ask me to mow the grass soon. I wouldn't know the first thing about mowing or using a lawn mower. I don't even know how to turn it on or anything.

I take all the clothes off the line and throw them into the basket, then stomp back inside and place the basket of clean clothes by the couch.

'Of course, sis,' she says to the phone. 'It's hard for a lot of first-time parents.' Aunty Dawn volunteers for some special helpline just for Aboriginal people that you call if you're depressed or suicidal. She signed up for it when she decided she was bored with retirement.

I head up the hallway, plug my dead phone into its charger and bluetooth some music to my speaker. I close my eyes and listen to Kendrick Lamar.

Two knocks spring me from near-sleep, my door creaks open and Aunty Dawn steps inside. She comes over and sits at the foot of my bed and I turn the music down.

'Anything you want to say to Aunty?' she asks.

I hate apologising, but I gotta do it. 'Yeah. I'm sorry.'

'Sorry for what?'

'I'm just sorry, you know. Sorry for the smokes. And for yelling at you.' I sigh. 'And I'm sorry for calling you a bitch.'

Aunty Dawn sighs too. She takes her phone from her pocket. She's probably the only person in Dalton's Bay who still uses a flip-phone.

'I need to tell you something,' she says. 'Well, *two* things. First, I ran into your English teacher at the shops. Mr Bartlett?'

'Mr Barrett,' I say. Mr Barrett's this tall guy in his fifties with an excellent blackish-grey ponytail and a grey goatee. He'd look like a wizard if he wore the right hat.

'He mentioned you got *one hundred per cent* on your writing assessment last week,' Aunty Dawn says.

'Oh, that was nothing.'

'He said your creative writing was *engrossing*, and he told me you have a *creative flair*,' Aunty Dawn says, smiling.

'Nah, I wish,' I say, almost blushing. I want to bury my head in my pillow. 'Barrett's been eating shrooms or something. It was just a fluke.'

'Fluke or not, you should be proud of yourself,' Aunty Dawn says.

'Mmm.'

Aunty Dawn clears her throat and shuffles an inch towards me on the bed.

'The other thing is: I got a call this morning – a call from your mother.'

I sit up. We haven't received a call from Mum or Dad since I was twelve, I reckon.

'Mum called? What did she want?'

'Umm,' Aunty Dawn begins, sucking her lips in, like she's trying to think of the best way to say what she's about to say. 'She was calling about your father. He's a bit sick, she said.'

'Sick?'

'Cancer, she reckons.'

I suddenly feel all hot. My heart is beginning to race.

'She said your father wants to see you again.' Aunty Dawn brushes some of my hair to the side of my forehead. 'Before it's too late.'

'Before it's too late?'

'Yeah,' Aunty Dawn says. 'Reckons he doesn't have much time left.'

'I don't want to see him,' I say, resting back on my pillow.

Aunty Dawn just gives me one of those smiles of hers that says *okay, I'll just leave you alone for now and ask again later*. She gets up from my bed.

'Think about it, bub,' she says. 'It's your decision to make.'

I roll onto my side. Her words linger in my ears – the soft and almost sighing way she said them: *Think about it, bub…It's your decision to make.*

There's nothing to think about, though. My mind is already made up. And I can't sit here in this room all night. I can't keep thinking about it.

I text Dally: *Coming over, I'll walk to the footy with ya.*

Dally replies: *Sweet no worries, Lenny's on his way.*

I pull on a shirt, then my red hoodie and slip into my Air Max. I lock my bedroom door and head to my windowsill. I gently open the window, put my leg through the opening and then slide my whole body out. Aunty Dawn's got a key to my room and she'll know I've sneaked out eventually, but I don't care. I need to be busy tonight.

I walk quickly for the bush. Once I'm behind the trees, I walk through the fallen sticks and crunchy leaves until I get to the driveway. I plug in my headphones and start 'Cinderella Man' by Eminem.

It's cold and windy on this Friday night. The trees around Aunty Dawn's house and along her driveway always sing when it's windy. They know I'm breaking the rules. They sing louder as if they're calling out to Aunty Dawn to snitch on me. They stand, watching me, as I head along the dirt driveway, a burning orange blanket of clouds lining the sky behind them.

I'm thinking about Dad. His face was round, and he always had a five o'clock shadow, curls dangling over his forehead, a freckle on his neck. I don't remember the sound of his voice.

I had my head out the window, looking back at the dirt road we were driving along, watching the dusty cloud our car was leaving behind. The road was crunching gravel loudly under our tyres when Dad took me and Trey out bush for the last time. A couple of the Uncles came with us and we drove to a clearing. Trey helped Dad put up the tent.

'You need to hammer that peg further into the ground, Trey,' Dad said loudly. Trey scoffed and used his shoe to push the metal peg right into the dirt.

Dad went over to the cars where the Uncles were unpacking. They opened a blue esky, and each pulled a beer from the ice inside. I used to think they were drinking poison, because that's what it smelt like to me and it always made Dad angrier when he drank it.

When the three tents were all ready, Dad and the Uncles grabbed fishing rods and we headed to the beach. Trey had a little fishing rod for himself, but I didn't.

We walked right up the beach and climbed onto the rocks. Everyone threw their lines in and sat there, but I couldn't sit still. I stepped into a rockpool. I found a starfish – I hadn't believed they were real before. The starfish was purple, so I pulled it out of the water and climbed over the rocks, back to Dad.

'Look, Dad,' I said. 'I found Patrick the starfish.'

'You know Dad doesn't like you interrupting him when he's fishing,' Dad said. 'Fishing is Dad's time to sit quietly in peace.'

I sat down on the rocks beside him and placed the starfish in a rockpool by my feet. It was more shallow than the one I'd found him in, but at least he was back in sea water.

A wave crashed into the rock beneath us and splashed us, hard. I wiped the spray from my face and saw Trey stand and walk further along the rocks. He readied himself, then cast his line into the water.

'Is Trey becoming a man now?' I asked Dad. I was six then and Trey was twelve.

'What do you mean?' Dad sighed, holding his fishing rod between his knees.

'I saw he's got hair under his armpits,' I said. 'And he's got some hair on his face, like he's growing a beard. Does that mean he's becoming a man?'

'It just means he's getting old,' Dad replied. 'Getting older doesn't make you a man. There are plenty of older people who act like little kids. It's a moment that makes a man. A decision. It's that moment when he grows on the inside. It doesn't matter how much hair a fulla has on his face. You don't become a man until you have that moment, when you make that decision.'

'What kind of decision?' I asked.

'It's different for everyone,' Dad said. He stood up from the rocks smiling, then began to reel in his fish.

3

I feel the sea spray on my face right now. I wipe my cheek, but I find it's dry. I don't want to think about Dad. He talked to me about what it meant to be a man, but I'm a man now and he ain't here. He doesn't know me at all.

My heart is pumping like a bass drum. I shake my head and focus on my steps. One step after the other.

It's a fifteen-minute walk along the dirt road until I'm on the bitumen and walking into the south side of Dalton's Bay. I pass by the lonely streetlight and head into the Valley – the few blocks on the south side are where all the poor white people and most of the Kooris live. I've always wondered why everyone calls these neighbourhoods the Valley, because it's not a real valley. Aunty Dawn once said that's where the government puts all the people they don't care about, which I thought at the time was a weird joke I didn't understand.

There are four people talking quietly by the fence near a little park with only two swing sets and a slippery dip. They're probably in their twenties and they look like Kooris.

21

I continue walking as 'Lose Yourself' begins in my ears. I've heard it too many times, so I skip it and listen to 'Walk on Water'.

Dally's house is right in the middle of the Valley on Orange Avenue. There are two dogs barking somewhere nearby – I can hear them when I turn my music down and pull the earphones out of my ears. Someone's listening to Elvis Presley on full volume, probably a few streets away. There's a car driving around nearby with a fucked muffler and it almost sounds like a truck. If this was a Saturday night I'd be worried, because on Saturdays the lads from the north side like to drive around the Valley and wind down their windows to call me and my mates shitty names. Sometimes, if they're in the mood, they'll get out and try to scare us. They reckon we're like rival gangs or something – *the boys from the Valley* and *the lads from the north*.

Dally and Lenny are waiting in the driveway when I get to Dally's house.

'Oi, bruz,' he says.

'Oi,' I reply. I should tell them about Dad, about the phone call, about the cancer, about him wanting to see me again. I thought him and Mum were gone from my life forever, but suddenly they're not. I should tell Dally and Lenny, but then I'd have to talk about it, about them, about how I feel.

'We're gonna be late,' Dally says.

'Yeah, let's get going,' I say. I decide to keep my mouth shut about my parents. I don't want to talk about them, I don't want to think about them.

I focus my thoughts on something else: this is my last walk into town with Lenny. He's leaving Dalton's Bay on Monday and moving to Sydney and it's all his sister's fault. She's been accepted into some acting school, so the whole family's moving up there with her. It makes me so depressed to think about him going. It was always just me, Dally and Lenny growing up. Dally and Lenny have always been like brothers to me – more than my real brother, Trey, who's living in Sydney last I heard. I've only seen him like twice since he moved out of Aunty Dawn's place when he was sixteen – the same age I am now. The last time would have been two Christmases ago. He drove down and visited for a couple days, then he was gone again. We're not as close as me, Dally and Lenny, that's for sure.

It's dark by the time we get into town. There are some kids at the basketball courts beside the youth centre and cars are lined up along the main street to get into the rec grounds for grand final night.

'Oi, boys,' I hear, then I sigh when I see it's Andy in his white hoodie. He's with four of the boys at the skate park, just beside the rec grounds. They come over from the park bench and together we all walk for the gates.

'How mad was camp?' Andy says. 'So mad being out bush with Travis and the brothers. Makes me feel like a fulla from the old days, choppin' up wood, making fires, fishing, washin' in the ocean water. Mad fun. You know what my favourite part about camping is? My hair still smells like the campfire for three days after.'

'Right,' I say to Andy, just wanting him to stop talking. We pay our five bucks each as we walk into the rec grounds.

'Stevie said he's over on the eastern side,' Dally says, reading a text from his phone.

Stevie's this older Koori fulla from the Valley who buys us grog sometimes. He's got his own place with his cousin and he has an Xbox and a blue heeler named Danger, so it's usually a good place to kick back. Aunty Dawn doesn't like him much, though. He dropped me off at home once and she started going off about how he's a *bad influence* and if I keep hanging with him, I'll end up going *nowhere* or some shit.

We start through the crowd, headed for Stevie's car. It seems like every person in Dalton's Bay is at the footy for grand final night. It's so cold that the grass is wet and slippery. As we make our way around the grounds, the lads from school appear, their sports bags looped over their muscular frames. Mark Cassidy walks in front. He's this big white lad who has somehow made the first-grade team this year. He's kind of like their ringleader.

Behind Mark is Porter Davis. He's this big-shot white kid, who reckons he's gonna be playing for the NRL soon, reckons that he's already been signed, or is going to sign, or an NRL club is interested in signing him, or something. He's a gym junkie, always posting photos on Instagram of himself at the gym or of his big tubs of protein powder. He's in Year Eleven with Mark.

'Watch it, dickhead,' Mark Cassidy says, dropping his shoulder into mine as he passes by. I turn to face him, but he keeps walking. The lads laugh and I want to shout something back, but I can't think of a good line and before long Mark and Porter and the others are too far away to hear me anyway.

We head around past the grandstands to the hill behind the goalposts. It's colder as we walk down the slippery, grassy hill, so I pull my hood over my head to warm my ears. The under-18s grand final is over, and the reserve grade teams are running onto the field right now. The hill is filled with a crowd of locals and supporters of the visiting teams. Dalton's Bay is hosting the grand final because the club installed a new digital scoreboard last year. It's got a countdown clock to time the games, which I imagine would be really annoying for the unfit players. I mean, I know if I was still playing footy, I'd hate nothing more than to be absolutely stuffed, and to look up and see twenty minutes and fifteen seconds left on the clock.

We walk along the other side of the footy field where all the parked cars flood the sideline and people have put down picnic blankets and chairs.

I spot Stevie's Commodore at the far corner, where the eucalyptus tree is monstered by the tall stadium light behind it. Jess is having a yarn with Stevie and Jye when we arrive, and Dally's quick to give her a hug. They've been having a kind of thing for a while, but now they're holding hands and they look like a real couple. Jess's friend Georgia is beside her, wearing a black hoodie and blue jean-shorts.

Stevie's got this new tattoo on the back of his hand of a saying in Latin that he refuses to tell us the meaning of. He got it done when he was last in Big Boys.

'Jamie,' Stevie says, shaking my hand. 'There's some VBs in the esky on the back seat, if you want one.'

I head to the car and slide onto the back seat. Lenny goes to the other side and we dig into the esky in the middle.

'Youse all ready for the move?' I ask.

'Almost. Mum and Elise headed up to Sydney this morning,' Lenny says. 'Me and Dad are gonna finish packing the van over the weekend and drive the rest up on Monday.'

I feel like making some joke or saying something funny like I usually do, but instead, I take another sip from my can of VB.

Georgia peers through the windscreen and our eyes meet. I look away. I've spoken to her maybe twice before and it's hard enough to talk to girls alone without trying to do it while all the boys are around. Usually I wouldn't have the balls, but tonight I feel like taking a risk.

I climb out of the car and head towards her. She's got a slight smile on her face as she watches the footy. She's so pretty tonight, with her red lipstick on. I pass her my VB. She takes a sip and coughs.

'Beer's fucked,' she says, handing the can back to me. Her breath is visible in the cold – a puff of white under the stadium lights.

'Yeah, I'm not a massive fan,' I reply. I shuffle beside her, leaning against the bonnet.

The reserve-grade grand final plays out. We watch from the car until the siren sounds at the end of the game. Cheers erupt in a small section of the crowd.

'I'm gonna head to the canteen if you want me to grab you a Coke?' I ask Georgia, as the presentations begin on the footy field.

'Yeah,' Georgia says. 'I'll come with ya.'

We head up to the canteen. Most of the spectators go there between games, so it's a long line we have to join. Georgia stands with me, and I feel like she's waiting for me to say something, start a conversation.

'You live with your aunty, yeah?' Georgia asks.

'Yeah,' I say. 'She's my mum's older cousin, so we're really *cousins*, I guess. I accidentally left my ciggies in my school shorts and she found 'em on Monday, so she was real pissed off about that. Now I'm on *thin ice*.'

Georgia giggles. 'So, she thinks you're like a proper smoker?'

'Yeah, I guess.'

The line is slow to move, but eventually we make it to the counter.

'You want a sausage sandwich as well?' I ask Georgia. She nods. I order two sausage sandwiches with onion and two Cokes, which somehow costs me sixteen bucks. Georgia tops off her sausage with tomato sauce, but I prefer barbecue.

The first-grade teams are running onto the field as we make our way through the crowd. We stop between two of the grandstands and eat our sandwiches.

'A bit overcooked, hey?' I sigh. Georgia nods. I'm feeling all awkward suddenly.

'Who you reckon's gonna win first grade?' Georgia asks.

'Probably Dalton's Bay,' I say. 'Would like to see 'em lose, though.'

'They're all arseholes.'

'Yeah. I would especially *love* to see Porter Davis lose.'

'Is he the one that reckons he's gonna play NRL?'

'Yeah,' I say. 'Number thirteen.'

'I've seen him around school. He's got nice calves,' Georgia says.

'Really? What about *mine*?' I ask.

Georgia checks out my legs slowly, the same way a scientist would examine a fossil.

She giggles again. 'You got no calves.'

'Go away, I *so* do.' I twist my leg out and flex my muscles as hard as I can. 'Just 'cause they're not muscly don't mean they're not there.'

Georgia laughs and pushes her shoulder into mine. I lean back and there is a flutter in the pit of my stomach.

I swallow the last of my sandwich and get started on the can of Coke as we make our way back to Stevie's car. My fingers are numbing from the cold of the can, so I pull my hoodie sleeve down and use it as a glove.

We get back to the car and now Dally's resting against the bonnet with fuck-buddy Jess lying back against him in his arms. *Not a couple,* he reckons.

Stevie and his cousin are standing at the sideline cheering on the Dalton's Bay Warriors. Stevie's drunk now, as animated as ever.

'Smash 'im, smash 'im,' Stevie shouts at every single tackle. 'Where you lookin', ref? Use those eyeballs in ya head!'

When Stevie comes back to his car, I'm sitting on the grass against the tyre. The ground is damp so my arse is getting wetter by the second, but I don't get up because Georgia sits on my lap. I'm suddenly not cold anymore as the weight of her body warms my thighs.

Two woman coppers with guns on their waists approach us, doing their rounds. They look us over, caught in their own private conversation. We're all dead quiet until they're gone. I imagine them deciding to drug search us, and they'd probably find something on Stevie and then arrest all of us on suspicion, then someone would film our violent arrest and they'd post it on social media, and there would be comments from old white people saying stuff like:

They shouldn't be breaking the law if they don't want to get arrested…

They're crims, they deserved it…

Cops went easy on them.

Stevie comes back and asks Dally for a cigarette and it reminds me of how angry Aunty Dawn was the other day. I've been a shit kid and I feel bad for swearing at her. She must be getting sick of me by now. It's annoying, when I feel bad like this. I don't like it. It makes me think about Mum and Dad, about Trey. It makes me think about how Mum has called Aunty Dawn saying Dad's dying, and how it's up to me to go see him so he can feel at peace or whatever.

'Can I get up?' I ask Georgia. She stands and I get another VB from the esky in the back of the car. I take a sip as I arrive back beside Georgia. I brush my hand against hers and her skin is cold. She doesn't stop me, just lets her fingers slip into the spaces between mine. Her eyes study our hands, connected, then they follow my arm up to my eyes and she stares. She's surprised. And I surprise myself when I lean in and kiss her. She kisses me back and it's nice and it's

29

brief before we turn our heads away. I can't help but smile. We keep holding hands and I take another sip of my VB.

'That was cute,' Georgia says.

'Yeah, well, I'm a cute guy. What can I say?'

Georgia giggles and squeezes my hand gently. Time doesn't really feel like it's happening anymore. The game on the footy field seems like a blur, but suddenly the full-time siren sounds and the Dalton's Bay Warriors have won the first-grade grand final. Porter Davis and his teammates are jumping around and screaming like they've just discovered the cure for cancer. Mark Cassidy is hugging his fat father-coach while the benched players are running onto the field to celebrate with the others.

Stevie, his cousin and a couple of the other boys get in the car.

'Drinks at mine,' he shouts out the window to us as he joins the chorus of cars crawling their way out of the rec grounds in single file. It's music to my ears, because I don't want to go home.

Me, Dally, Lenny, Georgia and Jess head for Stevie's place on foot. We leave the rec grounds with half the town, spill across the main street and hold up traffic. Two footy players without shirts on, in only football shorts and shoes, brush my shoulder as they rush past me.

'Jared's gonna meet us at the bottle-o, then Mark's having all the boys over for the afterparty,' one of the footy players says to the other.

Stevie's place is pretty packed by the time we get there. All of the boys are in the backyard doing shots of Jägermeister around the firepit. It's a pretty fresh winter's night, so the fire's welcome. Stevie's got a rock formation with three big boulders sitting together in the middle of his yard, before the incline grows steeper towards the back fence. Me and Dally sit on the rocks with Georgia and Jess, though I feel like we should be hanging out with Lenny. Lenny's over at the fire talking to one of the boys, telling 'em about his upcoming move. It's all making me kind of sad, so I drink some more grog and kiss Georgia again. I like being with her. She makes me forget about everything else for a minute.

By eleven o'clock, most people have headed home and the rest of us move to the verandah at the front of the house. It's just me, Dally, Lenny, Georgia, Jess, Stevie and his cousin left. Dally heads inside to get us more drinks and I find myself kissing Georgia in the corner of the verandah, away from everyone else.

'Wanna head inside?' Georgia whispers to me, and just when the words finish leaving her tongue, the sound of liquid hitting grass steals my attention across the verandah. Jess is spewing over the railing. Georgia rushes to Jess and holds back her hair while Jess hurls and hurls. And it's just my fucking luck that I finally get close to having sex with a girl and her friend spews and ruins it all.

'I better take her back to mine,' Georgia says.

'Wants us to walk you back? Me, Dal and Lenny?' I ask. Georgia nods.

It's freezing outside, and it's foggy down the hill towards the Valley. A car turns onto our street and the high beams come on as it nears us. The V6 engine roars. It speeds up and veers towards the five of us who are walking near the gutter on the side of the road. The horn sounds and the brakes screech as the car spins away. The windows are open. It's Mark Cassidy's new Mitsubishi sedan – the one his parents bought him for his birthday when he got his Ps.

'Junkiessss,' someone shouts out their window, laughing as the tyres spin and the back of the car swings towards us again. We all rush from the road and onto the grass. My heart is pounding out of my chest as I regain my balance and footing.

'What the fuck?' Dally shouts, puffing. 'Fucking dogs!'

Mark Cassidy's car speeds down the hill, then he slams on the brakes and spins back around. The car veers across the road towards us and the high beams come on, shining right into our faces.

The car screeches to a stop. Mark Cassidy's the first one out of the car and then Porter Davis. Two of the other lads follow and the four of them close in on us. Mark gives Dally a shove in the chest and he stumbles back and lands on his arse.

'Come on, junkie,' Mark says. 'Have a go.'

Porter and one of the lads grab Lenny, and Porter gets him in a headlock. I start for them, but Mark grabs my shirt. The other footy-head spits at my face.

'What the fuck!' Mark shouts. He lets me go and rubs his face with his shirt. I guess the footy-head got some of his spit on Mark as well. Dally gets up and pushes Mark, and he falls against his car. Mark comes back to me with real fire in his eyes.

Red and blue police lights stream into the sky from the bottom of the hill.

'Oh shit,' Porter says.

They all race to the car. Mark starts the engine and they speed off up the hill.

'What the fuck was that about?' Georgia asks, rubbing Jess's back as she has another spew in the gutter.

'Just dickheads,' I say, and my hands are shaky. 'Fucking dickheads.'

'I'm gonna kill them one day,' Dally says to me. He turns and power walks down the hill. The rest of us follow as the cop car flies past us and disappears.

4

It's about eleven o'clock when we arrive at the block of units where Georgia lives. The units are enveloped by fog, but I'm not cold anymore. I'm hot with anger.

Jess hugs us all goodbye and apologises for spewing, then Georgia takes her into the building.

We arrive back at Dally's house and sit down at the round table in his garage.

'Fuck those dickheads,' Dally says, taking a six-pack of beer out of the bar fridge. He throws a can each to me and Lenny. 'You right, Len?'

'Yeah,' Lenny says with a sigh, examining some blood on his elbow. 'Just a little cut.'

'We should really fuck 'em up,' Dally says, pacing around the garage.

'We'll get the boys together tomorrow and give 'em a go,' I say. I surprise myself. I don't like fighting, but I'm up for it. Those lads get around town like they own the place.

They look so far down on us, they don't expect us to really take it to them.

Dally springs up from his seat.

'I almost forgot,' he says. 'I got you a going-away present, Len.'

Dally rushes into the house and comes back, digging his nose inside a plastic sandwich bag. He holds it up to show us the greenery.

'What ya reckon?' Dally says. He passes the open bag to us, and Lenny and I take a whiff each: weed.

'What we gonna do with that?' I ask, knowing full well though I've never tried weed before.

'Smoke it, obviously. I found it in my brother's room earlier and got keen for the three of us to get high together before Lenny ditches us.'

Dally pulls a packet of papers from his pocket. He rolls the joint and he's first to take a drag. He draws back and coughs half his lungs up, sputtering like a newborn drinking milk for the first time. He hands it out to me and I place it between my lips and draw back. My mouth dries right up, and my lips grow numb instantly. I cough like a baby too, and I'm dizzy as I hand the joint over to Lenny. It is a strange dizzy, though. I'm not going to be sick or anything, but I am whirling in my seat.

'Damn,' I say.

'Look! Aunty Dawn's coming up the driveway, bruh,' Dally says, pointing behind me. My heart drops and I feel myself falling to hell as I turn around. But she ain't there, she's not coming up the driveway. Dally roars with laughter behind me. Lenny laughs along with him. The blood rushes hot through my veins and I think I might be having a heart attack. I can feel it all too, the muscles and tunnels surrounding my heart, my heartbeat travelling via some sort of chain up to my neck.

'Not funny,' I say, shaking my head. Dally and Lenny just continue to laugh. Lenny passes the joint to Dally and he has another draw. After I have had a moment to comprehend it was just a joke, and that it was actually pretty funny, I calm myself.

Lenny laughs. 'She'd give us a good floggin'.'

'Nah, she's too old for that these days,' I say. 'She'd just yell the walls down.'

Dally passes me the joint.

'You know,' he says, 'I think this is one of our *great nights*. One of those ones we'll look back on when we're older.'

'Okay, Gandalf.'

'Go away.' Dally laughs as he pegs the lighter at me. I catch it with a pretty impressive snatch. 'I don't want us to go our *separate ways*, you know?'

'I wish I was leaving tomorrow too,' I say.

'What? You abandoning me as well?' Dally asks.

'No,' I reply. 'I mean, you've got your apprenticeship, and now Lenny's going to Sydney…I'm gonna be a loner at school.'

'You got *Andy*, and the rest of the boys,' Dally says. 'Or you could drop out and get an apprenticeship like me.'

'Ha. I wish. Aunty Dawn wants me to do Year Twelve.'

Dally opens his second beer.

'You know you're smart enough to do it all, right?' Dally asks. 'School and uni, I mean. You're the smartest blackfulla I know.'

'No way.' I'm almost blushing.

'You could,' Dally says. 'You know the big words, and what they mean. You get good marks on your English stuff. You could really do something with that brain of yours if you wanted to.'

'Rightio,' I say. I take another draw from the joint as it gets passed around again. It's kind of weird hearing those words come out of Dally's mouth. They're nice words, unexpected. The weed's probably getting to him. 'You know what I *really* want to do?'

'What?' Dally and Lenny ask at the same time.

'I want to fuck up Mark Cassidy's car.'

Dally's eyes light like a fire and he sits up.

'Or we could just chill here for the night,' Lenny chimes in.

'Nah, Jamie's right,' Dally says. 'It's the perfect going-away present for you, Len. It's better than weed. You get to fuck up Mark Cassidy's car before you leave!'

'I dunno...' Lenny says, sinking back in his seat.

Dally sits forward and leans towards Lenny.

'Remember when we were doing that swimming assessment at the pool last year? The one where we had to go in the pool in all our clothes and tread water?' Dally asks.

'I dunno,' Lenny replies.

'When Mark said in the change rooms that he didn't wanna get in the same pool as the *abos*?' I ask.

Dally had a look in his eyes that day – a look that said shit was about to go down – right before he tried to beat Mark's brains out for saying that. I followed him and we both ended up getting suspended for a week.

'Yeah, and tonight…' Dally says. 'He's had it coming for a while. All of them have. He was probably heading home. I heard someone say they're having the afterparty at his place. His car will just be sitting in his driveway. What do you say, Len?'

'I dunno. It's a long walk to Vager's Drive,' Lenny says, looking to his feet. I know he's not much of a risk-taker. He just goes along with us when we do stupid shit.

'You'll be off to Sydney on Monday, anyway,' I say. 'It's not like he can chase after you or anything.'

Lenny takes a deep breath and sighs. 'Okay, fine. But if we get caught, I'm killing both of you.'

Me and Dally cheer and tap our beers together. Dally finishes off the joint and we take a fresh beer each for the road. We start for Mark Cassidy's house.

Dally slips his pocketknife into his pants. We walk back through the streets, over the hill and through the main drag into town. Opposite the bay, mountains stand in the far distance like giants watching over the town and the plains that lie between them and Dalton's Bay.

We walk to the north side of town, beneath the hills where my school is. Someone nearby is listening to the *Tenacious D* movie soundtrack from their little brick house. The music is so loud that even though we are across the street, we may as well be inside the lounge room. They are singing along, too, and they ain't good. Probably some late-twenties drunkard, just finished cleaning dishes at the RSL for the night, and thought they'd loosen up with some tunes.

Ahead on the corner of one of the streets is a public bench. There is a small group of people sitting under the shade of the big tree. The streetlight doesn't really illuminate them, but we can see the red glowing dots of the burning ends of cigarettes.

They're little kids, and they spot us as we near them, two of them ashing out their cigarettes. I can see them clearer now. They are the white boys in Year Seven, the ones who listen to Cardi B and Snoop Dogg and want to be gangsters. There are six of them. They like to mouth off at everyone at school, are always trying to start fights, swearing filthy at everyone. I've even heard they'd spent time down at the station – once when the cops found them out drunk and another time when they started a fight with an adult at the front of KFC. Public nuisance or something. They are no good. Good-for-nothings. Worse than even me and Dally. I kind of want to fight them just to knock some sense into their heads – so they would realise they aren't gangsters or hoodlums or anything like that; they are just kids who need to stop being little arseholes.

As we near the gutter opposite the bench the white boys are sitting on, a cop car appears from our left. We stay behind the hedges, step towards them to blend in with the darkness. The cops in the car shine their torches at the group of boys.

'You boys been hanging around the main street tonight?' one of the officers asks as the car comes to a halt. I know that voice: Senior Sergeant Hudson – he is as highly respected as they come. Got a few talking-tos here and there from him over the years. He likes to pull up beside you on the street and ask you what you're up to. And his white face is always in the paper: *Hudson's promotion* or *Hudson's birthday dinner* or whatever the new story is that month. He's even been to the community barbecues down at the Aboriginal health centre, showing his support for his local Indigenous community. He knows me. He knows all of us.

'Nah,' one of the kids says.

Me, Dally and Lenny back up. The two officers get out of the car and approach the boys. Dally climbs over the short front gate of the house on the corner. Without thinking, me and Lenny follow. It's exhilarating – the rush of the situation. Dally has his hand across his mouth, trying not to laugh. I do the same as I begin to chuckle. Lenny just looks scared and grasps his hair in a gentle pull.

The other copper speaks. He's a younger Italian guy – Officer Minelli. I remember he came to school with a woman copper for a presentation once. He complimented the dot painting I had done, which hung on the wall next to the painted cows and clouds and trees. I remember he even said he was a big admirer of Indigenous artworks.

The cops ask the boys what they're doing. They say they are just 'chillin'', 'hanging out'. They are probably shitting their pants as the officers ask to see their IDs, and search their pockets, and tell them to get their stupid arses home because it's bedtime.

As the cop car starts its engine and drives away slowly, I begin to worry that the person who lives in the house

40

on the corner will come outside for some reason or look out their window and see us on their lawn, crouching behind their hedges. They'd call those cops and have them right back.

We climb over the little front fence. Lenny is last and he kicks the gate, rattles it. The gate clangs like clash cymbals.

'Fuck,' Lenny whispers.

Me and Dally nearly piss ourselves laughing as we bolt across the street. We find ourselves coming into the laneway between Watson Street and Vager's Drive, Mark Cassidy's neighbourhood.

Me and Dally are laughing so hard now that we have to hunch over and hold our stomachs, trying to stop any sound from coming out of our mouths. Lenny limps into the laneway and shines his phone torch over his ankle. A small cut is bleeding just above the joint.

'Fucking stings,' Lenny says.

'Just put some spit on it,' Dally says.

'Spit?'

'Yeah, saliva's good for that. Cuts and stuff. Heals 'em right up.'

'That's ridiculous.' I giggle. I've never heard of that treatment before.

'Nah, for real. I swear it works. Saliva's good for cuts, I promise,' Dally says. It all seems like gibberish to me, but Lenny gathers some spit on the tips of his fingers and rubs it onto the cut.

After we get our breaths back, we head on to Vager's Drive. It's quiet, which has been the theme of the night.

'We're in the Vagina now. If you see a car coming, just dive into the nearest yard,' Dally says. 'Hide behind a bin or something.'

Our next stop: Mark Cassidy's house. From the street, I can hear the music and yelling and laughing from the footy afterparty.

Vager's Drive is the home of all the two-storeys, the three-storeys, the double garages, where the lawns are wide and the grass is kept short and green. The houses are all orange brick and big and, in the driveways, you can usually find a nice car or jeep or even a boat under a cover on a trailer. The road is wider on Vager's Drive, even though there are always only a couple of cars parked on the street. Mostly, the driveways are wide enough to accommodate any visitors or drop-ins. Cops never really patrol Vager's Drive. No Kooris live here.

'This will do nicely,' Dally says as he picks up a medium-sized rock from the gutter.

'I'm gonna kick off his mirror. Let's dent his doors,' I say to Lenny.

'Yeah,' Lenny says. 'And break off his bumper.'

We pass a few more houses along Vager's Drive and I see it there – Mark Cassidy's Mitsubishi – at the end of his driveway, parked behind his dad's BMW.

We approach Mark Cassidy's house and my heart is beginning to race. We're about to break the law. We're about to become *delinquents*.

'Nah, let's turn back. There's too much light out here, we got nothin' to hide our faces,' I say.

'Relax, don't worry,' Dally says. 'It's like midnight, too late for anyone to notice anything – their music's too loud in the backyard.'

Dally springs ahead of us, crosses the road and makes his way towards the Mitsubishi in the driveway. He drops the rock onto the well-kept nature strip, pulls out his pocket-knife and readies the blade.

'Say goodbye to your air, Markie-boy,' Dally says. He stops at the car tyre as me and Lenny step off the road and onto the driveway.

Then Dally gets that look in his eyes – the look that says *shit's about to go down*. Maybe I'm just high, but he seems to be brimming with excitement.

He waves us over with a strange smile. There, inside the car, still in the ignition, are the keys.

Car keys.

Keys for Mark Cassidy's Mitsubishi.

'Nooooo,' I whisper.

'Come on. We'll just take it for a quick spin. Dump it somewhere easy and he can have it back after,' Dally says. 'Fuck the fat bastard.'

I hardly have time to think about this before Dally has opened the driver's door and climbed into Mark Cassidy's Mitsubishi.

5

'We're not really doing this, are we?' Lenny asks.

'Get in,' is all I can say, because Dally starts the engine of Mark Cassidy's Mitsubishi. Lenny is quick onto the back seat and I follow him.

We reverse out of the driveway.

I struggle to pull my seatbelt across my body.

Car out of reverse and into drive.

Dally starts driving forward along Vager's Drive, then slams on the brakes.

'What the fuck? One of youse get in the front with me,' Dally says.

Lenny will probably die if he gets in the front. I just want us to get the fuck away from Mark Cassidy's house, so I crawl over into the front passenger's seat. Dally starts speeding up as I buckle myself in.

'Take it easy, you're going too fast,' I say. The V6 engine roars and Dally kicks the brakes. The seatbelt holds me, but

I jolt forward with the brake, then sling back into the seat. Dally just howls with laughter.

'Stop stressin',' he says. He eases his foot onto the accelerator, and we turn out of Vager's Drive at a normal speed – Dally even uses the blinker.

We are slow along the streets of town, just sticking to back roads and avoiding the main drag. Another car passes by at the intersection ahead. My stomach drops because it looks like a paddy-wagon, but it's just some old guy in a ute. Dally turns a corner.

'All right, that was good fun,' I say. 'Now let's drop it off somewhere and go back to your place.'

Dally doesn't respond or react at all. He keeps his eyes ahead, face steady, that look still in his eyes.

'Dally.'

He turns to me and I can almost feel Lenny's heart racing in the back seat. I'm sweaty all over; the backs of my knees, the palms of my hands.

'Not yet,' Dally says, almost sounding annoyed. He switches on the stereo as we come to a red traffic light. Music begins to blast from the speakers and Dally is quick to turn it down.

'Is this Justin Bieber?' I ask. 'I think I've heard this song on the radio.'

'Yep. This is one of his older albums,' Dally says. 'Mark Cassidy loves the Biebs.'

The three of us piss ourselves. We lose it as we drive along in the stolen car. The blood has rushed to my face and

I can't picture Mark Cassidy listening to a Bieber song and enjoying it.

'Now I got some ammo,' I say, and I can't wait to tease Mark Cassidy about being a Bieber fan.

The light turns green and Dally starts to ease across the intersection. I buzz down my window and look to my left. Slowing into the stop light is a cop car. Sitting there in the front passenger's seat is Sergeant Hudson. His eyes widen as he sees me seeing him. My finger is quick to the button and the window is back up in a few seconds, but I was too late. He's recognised me.

'Fuck,' I say. We start onto another street. I swing around in my seat and the belt burns my neck because of how quick I turn. *Please*, I think, *please don't*. But they do. The cop car turns in behind us. The red and blue lights come on and spray the houses and the convenience store as we pass by. They spray inside Mark Cassidy's car and the cop car speeds up behind us. Dally gasps and I think my life is over.

Fuck.

Dally is jittery as the blue and red lights flash into the car, then his foot falls flat on the accelerator. He jets ahead and drifts around the corner. Lenny and me are flung about in our seats. The seatbelt is tough against my chest, retracted and tight. The cop car comes around the corner behind us, picks up speed again.

We are speeding now, well and truly. We pass the young white boys the cops hassled earlier. They look and point and then they are gone as we zoom around another corner. I'm going to be sick. I'm in some kind of horror movie.

'Not today,' Dally says, eyeing the rear-view mirror. He speeds up, goes even faster. Another car almost comes into our path, but the driver spots us and slams on the brakes so quickly that it feels like the car's arse jolts upward for a second. Dally turns another corner and the heat inside me is at its peak. All the while, Justin Bieber continues blasting from the speakers.

Justin Bieber will be the soundtrack of our getaway.

Dally slams on the brakes as we turn onto the main street of Dalton's Bay. The tyres of Mark Cassidy's Mitsubishi spin and we slide into the right lane. Then the V6 engine roars and we are off again. The sirens are after us now, they are louder than the music and punch through the closed windows.

The thought comes to me: *this is how I die.* Dally is going to lose control of the car and crash us into a pole or a house and we will all be killed on impact.

'Dally, that's enough,' I say, defeated. I turn back to see the cop car racing after us, twenty or thirty metres behind. 'Just give it up. We're done!'

'Fuck that,' Dally says. He pushes harder on the accelerator. The shops blur as we pass them. I am definitely going to be sick.

The road is clear ahead, but I know it will only take one person crossing the street, one dog roaming into our path and we will be dead. I will know I'm going to die before it actually happens.

The tyres screech as we drift around another corner. Dally is panting now. The road becomes rough and I bounce up and down in the passenger's seat. My head whacks the roof and starts throbbing. We hit the dirt. The darkness ahead is broken only by the beam of the headlights as we pass over rocks and shrubbery. Dally switches on the high beams and a metal fence reveals itself. Before I can even process the sight of it, Dally blasts us through the fence, busting it open. The fence bashes at the sides of the car, a chain cracks the windscreen and it sounds like a blast from one of those guns the Stormtroopers use in *Star Wars*. Dally turns right, we bust through another fence and I know we have just destroyed the Dalton's Bay water tower's protective barriers.

We thud onto a smooth road and glide along. Dally has to lean a little to his right to see, avoiding the big crack in the centre of the windscreen.

'Fuck me,' I say, breathless.

The blue and red lights are still behind us, the car moving from right to left. The cloud of dust is settling. Dally switches the car's headlights off. Ahead now there is only darkness except for the distant white glow of a streetlight.

'It's dead straight until that light,' Dally says, also breathless. 'We'll turn onto Harrison's Road and then the bushes will hide us.'

I place my hands on my chest. I'm breathing so fast I think my lungs might explode. My hands are shaky and wet. I'm scared for my life.

I turn back to Lenny. His forehead is glistening with sweat and, as he locks eyes with me, he vomits. I hear it slushing onto the back floor of Mark Cassidy's Mitsubishi.

The foul smell fills the car, so I bring my window down again. Dally hunches forward, eyes wide, staring at the light ahead growing nearer as wind fills the car. I think about kangaroos and wombats. We wouldn't see them in time to brake.

Behind us, there's a set of headlights. It must be the cop car. They have turned off their reds and blues, getting closer as Dally eases off the accelerator and the car begins to slow down. We are almost at the streetlight now. My heart starts racing again because I can't see anything else except the pole and the light at its top. I know that if Dally fucks up the turn, we will go head-on into the pole or a tree.

'I got this,' Dally says. He veers to the left to keep to the night's darkness. He knows if we come too much under the light, the cops will see us there for that moment before we turn, and they will know where we are going.

It's a sharp turn and my eyes are closing tight again. I await the pole or the tree as we travel onto dirt and bumps. The sound of the road is as deafening as the roar of the V6 engine when Dally hits the accelerator again. I open my eyes and there is nothing but black. True black.

'The lights!' I shout.

'Not yet.'

We are slow at first, but our speed is picking up. I shake my head because I can't close my eyes again.

Dally flicks the headlights on and we are driving straight along Harrison's Road. The bush is dense around us. The branches of the arching trees hang down and graze the roof. I picture all the scratches on the car, the dents, all the money

Mark Cassidy will try to get from us for the damage even though we have nothing. His parents could cover it and it wouldn't have any impact on their finances. We would never be able to pay for it.

I look out the back window as we keep on straight. No headlights behind us. No blue and red. The road turns as we pass around the underside of the mountain, the one that seemed like a distant giant earlier and is now helping us hide. A smaller road appears on the right and Dally slows into the turn.

'That's enough, Biebs,' I say as I switch off the stereo. Dally cracks up again, laughing like a maniac. Lenny follows Dally's lead, snorting his snot back inside as he laughs. We come to the Dalton's Bay River. Although it is mostly dry now, I can see a steady stream with the aid of our headlights, maybe knee-deep, flowing along the very centre of the river.

Dally brakes and pulls into a space between two thick bushes. He puts the car in park and switches off the engine. The lights come on inside the car. Dally unbuckles his seatbelt, lets out a big sigh and we all get out of the car.

'That was fucked, man,' Dally says.

'Ya reckon?' I chuckle as we lean against the side of the car.

'Oi, dickheads,' Lenny says. 'I'm moving to Sydney on Monday. Remember? I can't get fucking arrested tonight. I can't die tonight, either. Fucking hell.'

'Calm down, bruh,' Dally says.

Lenny just shakes his head and starts for the edge of the Dalton's Bay River.

'Where you going?' I ask Lenny.

'Home. I'll walk 'cause there's no way I'm getting back into a fucking stolen car.'

'Wait.' Dally starts walking towards him. 'Wait.'

Lenny turns around. Even though it's dark, he looks like a tortured puppy who just wants to go home and sleep.

'I'm sorry, Lenny,' Dally says. He reaches his arm around Lenny's shoulder and directs him back to me and the car. 'We'll head around through the bush. I know a way that brings us to the footy fields. Might be a bit rough in this thing, but we'll leave the car there and walk the rest of the way. Sound good?'

Lenny sighs, then he nods, just like he always does whenever Dally and me are doing something stupid. Lenny always seems to get dragged along. We never force him to follow us, he still comes anyway.

We rest our backs against the car as we sit on the grass and dirt. The night is even colder now.

'Some last night out.' Lenny chuckles.

'When you're in Sydney, when the city fullas ask you about leaving DB,' Dally says, 'you can tell 'em your last night with your mates was fucking hectic.'

Lenny chuckles, then he goes quiet again. For a moment, it's just the crickets and the mosquitos I hear. Then I remember Hudson's face, staring at me from the cop car before I could buzz the window up. He saw me, he recognised me. No matter what else happens tonight, *I'm* fucked.

'I'm really gonna miss you guys.' Lenny sighs. 'I mean it. You're my brothers.'

I turn to him. His dark face is half-lit by the moonlight. I can see there are tears threatening to leak from his eyes. I might even cry myself.

'We love ya, you silly bastard,' I say. 'Although when Mark finds your vomit on the back seat, I think he's gonna go all the way to Sydney to kill ya.'

We all laugh and it feels like we are ten years old again, watching some Adam Sandler comedy on Dally's floor, lying on the three single mattresses pushed together because we have to share the blankets.

'I'll come back to visit when I can,' Lenny says. 'Jamie, you'll probably be on welfare, bumming around the youth centre for a feed.'

'Fuck off.' I laugh.

'And Dally, you'll probably be in and out of prison,' Lenny says. I just cough and laugh so hard. Dally takes Lenny in a headlock. They play-fight, like they are real brothers. I'm glad to be a part of these moments – moments when I can forget I'm stuck in a house with Aunty Dawn and Uncle Bobby, when I can forget my father wants to see me again.

Dally and Lenny join me back on the ground by the car. They are both puffed. Dally pulls his bag of weed from his pocket and opens the car door. He kneels on the ground and rolls a joint on the front seat.

'Surely not,' I say.

'Surely yes,' Dally replies.

'You really think that's a good idea?'

'Yeah, *you're* driving back,' Dally says.

'Like hell I am,' I reply. 'No way.'

He lights the joint and we pass it around. I only have one puff because I am high again instantly. When the joint is finished, Dally flicks it over to the river.

'We fucked up.' Dally chuckles. I can't help but chuckle a little myself too. 'But you know what? That drive was the most fun I've ever had.'

'Really?' I ask.

'Speak for yourself,' Lenny says.

'No, it was.' Dally sits forward and glances over me and Lenny. 'We should do it again sometime.'

'I think not,' I say.

We laugh again. The rush of what we've done is wearing off and a chill is settling over my body. My arms are numb, so I rub them. I relax my back against the car and take in a breath. The air is fresh and clean and light. The trees speak to each other with the breeze, just gentle leaves brushing against each other. I could close my eyes and fall asleep, but my throat is dry and I have to lick my lips to stop myself from thinking I am going to choke to death from the weed.

'Do youse remember when we were at Aunty Dawn's sixtieth?' Dally asks.

Me and Lenny nod. We were probably seven or eight then.

'Do you remember when we had to take her blue heeler for a walk because she was constipated? What was her name again?' Dally asks. 'Rosy? Roly?'

'Roxy,' I say. 'She was old and she sure looked it.'

'Wasn't she blind in one eye? And her tail had like no fur at all.' Lenny sits up and smiles, like he has gotten some spurt of energy.

Dally continues, 'Yeah, she looked like she went through a meat grinder and lived to tell the story. We took her for a walk down in the bush, around the walking track, so she could shit. We didn't know anything.'

'What you mean?' I ask.

'I mean we had no idea about life, you know? We didn't know about growing up, or money. We didn't know we were poor or anything like that. We were just these kids walking this old dog in the bush so that she could shit. Nothing else mattered except what we were doing at that moment.'

'No more weed for you,' I tease.

Dally smiles and shakes his head. 'I just want to go back to those days,' he says, placing a cigarette in his mouth. 'When—'

'Stop,' Lenny interrupts. He sits up, his ears perked like a meerkat's. 'Listen.'

Dally holds the unstruck lighter to the end of his cigarette.

I listen. The crickets are about, and the breeze is still rolling through the trees. Then I hear it: a rumble. An engine. Tyres against gravel. A weak light flickering against a tree across the road.

We spring to our feet. My whole body is shaking. A coat of sweat covers my skin.

'Fuck,' Dally says.

'We gotta run,' I shout.

'No, get back in the car,' Dally says, launching himself into the driver's seat. Lenny climbs onto the back seat and I race to the front passenger's seat.

'Maybe it's not even the cops?' I say.

'It's them,' Dally replies.

'Maybe they won't see us,' Lenny says. 'We're hidden, right?'

'Not hidden enough,' Dally says, igniting the engine and jolting the car into reverse. The headlights come on and he shifts the car into drive. We speed back along the road and all I can do is fasten my seatbelt.

I look back through the rear window. A spotlight comes shining around the far corner, cutting through the cloud of dust we are leaving behind. Lenny is near tears.

'Fuck!' Dally shouts.

He brakes and we make a sharp turn as the road winds around the side of the mountain. We slide across the dirt and the rear of the Mitsubishi scrapes the bank. The tyres spin as Dally accelerates again. But we are stuck. The spotlight behind us is getting closer, then the red and blue begins to flash again. The sirens follow.

'Come on,' I say.

Dally turns the steering wheel right and the car begins to edge forward. Only the dirt road can be seen out of the windscreen, but Dally keeps accelerating and then we are off and back on the road. The engine is sounding sick now, almost coughing along.

I have no idea where the hell we are going. I haven't been on this road in years, least of all at night.

'Just pull over, Dal,' I say. 'We'll make a run for the bushes. We'll get away.'

'We won't,' Dally shouts back. For the first time tonight, I hear fear in his voice. It worries me, because if he's worried about a situation, our hopes are dire.

The road becomes bumpier and rougher beneath us. Dally keeps to his speed as he takes the turns and weaves, and we head uphill. The lights of the cop car are receding behind us. Maybe the dust is deterring them. Maybe their still-shining spotlight isn't so powerful after all.

Dally takes a sharp right turn onto another dirt road, with a big signpost blurring as we narrowly miss it with the rear of the car. Dally switches to low beam again and eases his foot off the accelerator. He is panting like a dog on a hot day, thirsty for water.

I look behind us and out the rear window again. No lights except for our red tail-lights, and then there is just darkness and dust and the banks of the narrow road we are driving along.

'I think we lost 'em,' I say. Pretty much as soon as the words come out of my mouth, the spotlight appears again.

'Fuck,' Dally shouts. 'You'd think with all the money fat Cassidy has, he'd at least put some fucking petrol in the car.'

I gaze over to the dashboard. The fucking car is about to run out of petrol.

'Come on,' I say, pleading now. 'We need to just get ourselves some distance, stop the car and run.'

'We'll never find our way back in the dark,' Dally says.

'It's better than getting fucking locked up, isn't it? And you know they won't just put the cuffs on us, they'll rough us up too.'

Dally hangs his head for a moment, then glances at the rear-view mirror. I turn around to see the red and blue lights gaining on us.

'Hold on then, boys,' Dally says. He turns up the music. Once again, we have Justin Bieber as the soundtrack to our night. We drive faster and faster. I grip the armrest on my door and hold it as tight as I can. My hands are slippery and sweaty. I don't want to look back to Lenny and see the horror on his face, so I just look forward through the cracked windscreen, as we bump and swerve our way along the dirt. The trees are tall around us and I imagine they are cheering us on.

'Oh, fuuuuuck!' Dally shouts.

A kangaroo has hopped onto the road.

So big. So close.

Dally rises in his seat, puts all of his weight onto the brake pedal.

We hit it with the front right headlight.

The impact makes a bang like a shotgun blast.

The airbag pops, whacks me in the nose.

Everything is black for a moment.

Then, throbbing.

Blood gushing from my nostrils.

We swerve around and around.

It's like I'm on the Cha Cha at the Dalton's Bay Carnival.

My stomach's in a freefall.

The back of the car smashes into the bank and we jolt forward.

The airbags deflate.

Breathe in and out.

Breathe in and out.

Breathe in and out.

Open my eyes. Vision is blurry.

Our headlights' beam flickers over the road.

Dirt and new cracks on the windscreen.

Red and blue flashes on the roof and on the door.

Coughing beside me.

It's Dally coming to.

He pushes the airbag away from his body, back to the steering wheel, but he is sluggish. Lenny's arms are shaking as he grips the back of my seat with all his might, arms extended, his hair drooping from the sweat.

My head is aching like I've just been punched. I'm dizzy, stars twinkle across my vision, and Justin Bieber is still singing.

6

Dally tries the accelerator. We jolt forward, then chug to a roll, but the engine dies.

'Come on,' Dally says. 'We gotta get goin'.'

I grab his arm after he unlatches his seatbelt's buckle.

'Cuz,' I say. My voice is croaky and sore. 'They got us.'

Dally turns around and looks through the back window, his face bathed in the flashing blue and red lights. They are right behind us. Dally exhales and swallows and I see the hope fall from his eyes right before the spotlight comes on again and blasts into them. He winces and falls back against his seat.

'I'm sorry, Lenny,' Dally says. 'I couldn't get us out of it.'

'It was the fucking kangaroo,' I say. 'Not *your* fault.'

'All right, that's enough, fellas.' Sergeant Hudson's voice rings out, projected from a speaker. 'Step out of the car one by one with your hands in the air.'

I look to Dally. His face has lost its colour. He rests his head against the deflated airbag. I turn back through the blinding spotlight to face Lenny. He is shaking in his seat and looks like he's about to faint.

'You know what we have to do,' I say. Dally looks up to me, tears welling in his eyes. 'We have to distract them, cause a scene. Lenny can get away, then. He won't get in trouble.'

'They'll kill us,' Dally says. 'You know they'll kill us. We don't matter to them. They don't care about us. We're just black faces.'

I take a breath.

'Dal. You have to trust me. It's the only way Lenny can get out of this. You know how strict his parents are. They'll disown him.' I relax back in my seat. 'Yeah, we'll get roughed up a bit, but at least Lenny will get away.'

Dally looks back at Lenny. He sees Lenny shaking. He sees the fear in his eyes, how desperately he just wants to be on his way to Sydney with his family.

'You all right, Lenny?' Dally asks.

'Yeah,' Lenny says. His voice is soft and weak, like he's been screaming at the top of his lungs for an hour without a break.

'We'll distract them, and you run. Right?'

'I don't know,' Lenny says.

'You have to. Jamie's right. You don't deserve to be in this shit with us when you're so close to getting out of here. You just have to run into the bushes over that way.' Dally points to our right, towards Dalton's Bay. 'Just keep going until you get to the farms and fields. You got this, brother.'

Lenny looks like a frightened puppy dog, but he swallows hard and nods. Dally turns back to me and I release my seatbelt.

'You first,' Dally says to me.

I grip the lever in my sweaty hand, still high as a kite. I open the door and use my foot to push it out all the way.

'Hands in the air,' Sergeant Hudson orders.

I plant my foot on the dirt. I climb out slowly, straighten my back and hold my hands above my ears. Hudson orders me to turn around slowly to face them, so I do. The light is so bright and white that the red and blue flashes are hardly visible above it.

'Jamie Langton,' Hudson says. 'Walk towards me. Very, very slowly. Keep those hands up.'

I focus on my feet. I start walking, placing one foot in front of the other. I can feel the cool breeze. A sensation comes over me, of relief – relief that the ordeal is finally over.

I arrive beside the headlights of the cop car and Hudson orders me to stop walking. The passenger door opens. Minelli steps out.

'Turn around, Jamie,' he says. He sounds disappointed, or maybe he's exhausted himself. He looks older in the dark, but he is youngish. Late twenties, would be my guess. His olive skin is lighter somehow in the spill from the spotlight, as he stands there with cuffs in one hand and the other on his holster.

I turn around slowly. Minelli orders me to place my hands on the back of my head, so I do. I look back to Mark Cassidy's Mitsubishi. The rear bumper has come loose. There is dust all over the car and some liquid is leaking out near the exhaust pipe.

I can see the side of Dally's face and the back of Lenny's curly black hair, fluffed above the headrest of his seat.

I hear footsteps, then Minelli's hands come to my wrist. The handcuffs are cold as he latches them onto one of my wrists, then brings down my other hand and cuffs them together.

He yanks me back with a tight grip on my forearm. Then I'm on the back seat of the cop car. Minelli leaves the door open after I slip my legs inside. He turns his attention back to the Mitsubishi. I spot Sergeant Hudson's eyes through the window. They are wrinkled at their corners, like he is smiling.

'All right, next one out,' he calls.

I look ahead. The driver's door opens, and Dally steps out. Minelli crosses the front of the cop car and stands beside the car's front wheel.

Dally is ordered to do the same as me. He turns around, hands above his head. I watch as he slowly backs towards Minelli, who has Dally's handcuffs at the ready. I see Lenny slide across to the right door, behind the driver's seat. I imagine the adrenaline rushing through his body as he waits for us.

Dally makes it to the front of the cop car and Minelli orders him to stop. Dally places his hands against the back of his head, as ordered. I am careful and slow as I slide one foot towards the outside of the open door.

As Minelli latches one of the cuffs closed over Dally's left wrist, Dally turns, wraps his arm around Minelli and they both go down.

I fling myself out of the back of the cop car. My head is heavy and my balance is off. I stumble, but manage to get my legs back under me. I run into the blackness, the red and blue spilling over me. Hudson's heavy boots pound away on the dirt behind me.

And everything falls silent for a moment. I concentrate on my breaths, in and out, like a pumping sprinkler.

A bang on my back launches me to the ground. Hudson's shoulder. I slide along for a metre or so. The dirt grazes my face and it feels like my cheek is on fire. It hurts like hell, but I don't care, as long as Lenny has stuck to the plan and is getting away through the bush.

I'm pulled to my feet and thrown into the cop car. Dally's eye is purple when Hudson shoves him beside me on the back seat. He has blood on his forehead where the skin has been scraped away by the dirt. My stomach sinks when I see Minelli sprint into the bush.

Hudson looks at me through the window. 'Your aunty wouldn't be happy with you, Mr Langton.' He laughs.

'Fuck you!'

Hudson doesn't react.

'Fucking pigs,' Dally says.

'Quiet, boy,' Hudson says.

Dally nudges me with his knee, hunches forward on his seat with his hands cuffed behind his back. His eyes are glassy. I'm worried for Lenny. It's too dark in the bush. He won't be able to see where he's going.

'He's gonna get him,' Dally whispers to me with a sniffle. Dally shuffles and backs up to his door, reaches for the handle. Hudson has not left the side of the car. Dally pulls the handle, but the door is locked. He pulls and pulls, and the car begins to rock. The windows fog with our body heat. Hudson peers in at Dally for a moment with a smirk on his face, and Dally sighs.

It's hopeless. There is nothing we can do. We are fucked, and I could damn near cry my eyes out.

'Took your sweet time,' Hudson says. I look back through the foggy window to see Minelli forcing Lenny out of the bush and onto the road, his hands cuffed.

'It's going to be a tight squeeze in the back,' Hudson says, peering in at me and Dally again. He opens the door and Minelli shoves Lenny onto the seat. Dally wiggles into the middle.

'You blackfellas never learn,' Hudson says, shaking his head at us before he closes his door. 'Never learn.'

Lenny's puffing, but he doesn't say a word. Me and Dally don't say nothing either.

7

As we travel out of the bush in the back seat of a cop car, the trees somehow look different. The headlights shine on them, and I can see they are watching us, disappointed.

The dread comes over me in a layer of sweat and tiredness. I just want to get in my bed, pull the blanket up to my shoulders, but I am on my way to the police station. I'm going to be locked up.

I can see Lenny's parents disowning him. I can see Dally's father beating him near to death like he did when he was younger, when he would sometimes come to school with bruises and black eyes.

As we arrive back in town, I'm thankful no one is on the footpath to see my face staring out the back window of a cop car.

We come to the police station. The car turns up the driveway and the electronic gate opens for us. In the car park all the lights shine bright overhead, and two more coppers await us by the back entrance. A younger cop opens the back door of the police station and leans against it to keep it ajar.

As soon as the engine shuts off, Dally begins kneeing and headbutting the back of Minelli's seat.

'Fucking pigs,' Dally shouts.

Minelli mutters something.

He rips his seatbelt from its restraint.

He springs out of the car and opens the back door.

He pulls Lenny and Dally out of the car.

My door opens and Hudson pulls me out too.

Someone strong grabs my arms.

I bang against the back of the car.

Stomach first – winds me.

Copper's weight against my back.

Pinned.

The copper pushes so hard the air is squeezing right out of me.

Lenny is crying his eyes out.

'It's all right, cuz,' I shout. Lenny doesn't respond.

Dally resists.

Within seconds, he is on his stomach on the ground.

Minelli's hard knee is in the centre of his back.

Another officer plants his knee in Dally's back as well.

'Get the fuck off me!' Dally shouts, over and over. 'Get the fuck off me!'

I am crying too now.

Coppers shove me away.

Arms on my shoulders push me towards the police station, towards the opened back door.

I am shaking.

Shivering like I'm cold, but there is lava beneath my skin.

Dark night.

Stars are out but clouds hide them.

Warm breeze of a heater hits me.

Coppers walk me along a white corridor.

Over my shoulder, Lenny's being brought inside by another officer.

I don't see Dally.

They are beating him to death outside.

I'm shoved into a room.

Pushed towards a small cell.

No more than two metres in width and length.

A steel seat bolted against the back wall.

I'm uncuffed and the door is locked behind me.

I stand there against the glass, watch as Lenny is locked in the cell next to mine.

My whole body is sweating.

Blood rushing back through my wrists to my fingertips.

My hands begin to feel hot and tingly.

'Go fuck yourselves,' Dally shouts, his voice echoing through the corridors. The coppers drag Dally around the corner and into the room.

Dally's feet can't find the floor.

The coppers carry him by his shoulders and arms.

Four coppers are on him, Minelli included.

Dally's face is all bloodied.

His nose is big and red and purple.

They drag Dally past me and open the cell beside Lenny's. All the while, those handcuffs are still fastened around his wrists, now coloured red by Dally's blood. They remove the cuffs after they sit him down, then they close the door and the lock clicks into place. The four coppers who carried him in there all bloodied walk away, back the way they came. There is a woman copper, who I don't recognise, taking a seat behind the desk near the doorway.

My breathing steadies and I stand there at the glass. I can hear the woman copper's fingers hitting the keyboard of her computer as she types something. Heavy boots tap on the floor until they settle to quietness in the distance.

'Dally,' Lenny says. 'You right, cuz?'

The cop looks up from her desk and stares us down.

No answer. I can hear Dally panting, then he takes some deep breaths.

It stays quiet in the holding room until a black face appears at the doorway. He is tall and old and familiar with an unkempt grey beard. Uncle Ray, an Elder from Barton, an hour away by car. He's one of those old cultural Kooris, always doing barbecues and get-togethers with the mob and smoking ceremonies and speeches for the whitefellas. He wears a nice salmon-coloured shirt, buttoned and collared, and blue jeans, with a cowboy hat on his head. He looks like an Aboriginal cowboy. He walks over to us.

'You boys right?' he asks. Me and Lenny say 'yes'.

'Those pigs fucked me up,' Dally says.

'Jamie,' Uncle Ray says to me as he walks past my cell. 'Dally. And you, you're Lenny, right? I've spoken with the officers in charge and with your parents and carers. They will come first thing in the morning. It's two o'clock right now, so I'll stay here with you until your parents come in. Make sure youse feel safe, yeah?'

Dally and Lenny stay quiet. I don't bother responding. I don't think Uncle Ray really cares. He's probably just here for a few extra bucks. I don't know. I'm just annoyed he has propped himself on a chair on the other side of the glass of *my* holding cell. He's close enough to hear me breathe, I reckon, and close enough to smell my body odour.

I close my eyes. I remember Uncle Ray came over to Aunty Dawn's place one time, smoked out the whole place with his bucket of gumleaves. I think I was nine or ten then. I was pretty much huddling behind Trey the whole time because I was terrified when Uncle Ray started talking about *bad spirits* and *cleansing*.

I wake and for the briefest moment, the whole of last night feels like a dream. But I'm still in the holding cell. An officer walks into the room. Her footsteps on the cement wake Uncle Ray as well and he sits up and snorts.

'Their parents are here,' the copper tells Uncle Ray. I rub my eyes, and my hands are so sore.

The cops come in and take Lenny out of his cell in handcuffs. They handcuff me and whisk me away to a white room with a table in it. I wake up fully when I see Aunty Dawn sitting there at the table. She's got bags under her eyes and her hair is all frizzy. Her face seems more wrinkled somehow as our eyes meet. The officers sit me down. I expect them to take the cuffs off, but they don't. They leave the room and I'm just sitting here, tired and dirty, with my handcuffs tight around my sore wrists.

'You all right, Jamie?' she asks. I guess she can see the bruises on my face.

'Yeah. I'm all good.'

'Your caseworker, Lauren, is going to meet us at court.'

'So, I have to go to court?' I ask.

Like his white ears must've been burning, a detective comes in and sits with us. Aunty Dawn moves over to me. As the detective begins to talk, I look to my hands in my lap. My wrists have red rings around them. The cop tells me I'm charged with car theft and all this other shit that I don't really pay attention to. All I know is I have to go to court.

|||

Lauren almost trips over as she rushes into the court-room. She halts to do her little bow to the magistrate at the bench in front of us, then sits beside Aunty Dawn on the bench behind me. I stand on a platform with a wooden fence the height of my waist.

My legal aid, a younger man, probably late twenties or early thirties, sits beside me. He wears a grey suit and black tie. His hair is neatly combed to the side and his face is hairless, apart from his eyebrows. Seriously, the skin on his face is as hairless as a baby's arse. The magistrate starts to talk and my legal aid presents his arguments for *trauma* and *out-of-home care system* and *peer pressure* bullshit. The magistrate has a build-up of saliva in the corners of her lips and claps her wet mouth when she talks.

'Danger to the community...High severity...Troubling...Reckless...Bad influence...'

She probably thinks her words hurt me, but they hardly leave a bruise. She tells me bail is refused. The court officers take me away in my handcuffs. They walk me through a door and through another door and another and then I'm in another holding cell.

Lauren comes waddling behind the legal aid. Her heels click loudly on the hard floor. They both pull some seats from against the wall and sit them at my cell. Lauren looks like she's just gone for a run. Her forehead is glistening from the overhead fluoro lights.

'James, how are you?' she asks.

'All good.'

I'm not all good, though. I'm tired. My cheek is itchy and hot. My back is sore. I want to see my mates again. I want to know that they're okay.

Lauren clears her throat, opens her folder and starts flicking through plastic slips filled with papers. She pulls out a piece of paper and starts scribbling, turns to the legal aid.

'Can you tell us what exactly is happening? I can never understand any of that legal talk.'

The legal aid sits up in his seat and starts to talk, but he's hard to follow. He's got a dull, boring voice. The only takeaway is that me, Dally and Lenny are getting locked up.

'Jamie's been refused bail. He'll be held on remand at Kinston Juvenile Justice Centre in Kinston City up the coast.'

'How long will he be there on remand?' Lauren asks.

'The judge has set a date for September twentieth.'

'That's a month away.' I chuckle. 'Fuck.'

'So, he just sits there until he's found guilty or not?' Lauren asks as she leans forward and rubs her temple.

'Do you understand what I've just said, James?' the legal aid asks.

'Yep.'

'You might have to wait it out for a while. Things move slowly in the legal world,' he says.

He talks to Lauren some more and she asks more questions and I'm starting to think she isn't smart. Or maybe she's just asking so many questions because she wants to get as much information as she can. I don't see why she cares so much. She's not the one who will be doing the time. And I know she can't actually like me. She's at work and she's getting paid to do her job, just like the caseworker before her and the caseworker before that one.

The handcuffs are looser on my wrists as the court officers take me away. They throw me in the bus and pull me back out when we get to the police station.

I'm taken to a small room and Aunty Dawn arrives. She stands by the closed door for a moment, studies the white walls of the room. I think she's probably trying to muster the courage to look at me. She must be so disappointed, fed up. She's about to rip me up like a roast chicken from Coles, tell me she's had enough.

'Oh, Jamie,' she says. She dawdles to the table and sits in the chair across from me. She places her hands on the surface and sighs. 'How are you feeling?' she asks.

She finally finds my eyes, but I can't look. I turn to the white walls like she did as I shrug my shoulders.

'It's okay to be upset or angry. This is a tough spot you're in.'

I shrug my shoulders again. She thinks she's failed me, but she didn't. It's just...I...I'm no good. I don't bring no happiness to anyone. I wish I could say it to her. I wish I could open my mouth and say it.

It's not your fault. I'm no good.

'You just keep your head up,' Aunty Dawn says. 'You keep your back straight and remember who you are. I might not be your mother, but you're my boy. You're my son. You'll always be. When you get to that place, you keep your head up. Remember how much me and Uncle love you. Don't let that place break you. You're stronger than the system. Stay out of trouble. Do your time. You'll be out before you know it. You'll be okay, Jamie.'

A tear is escaping my eye, so I quickly wipe it away. I don't want her to see it. I don't want her to know how scared I am. I don't want her to worry.

'Aunt. I'm all good. I'll be right, I swear.' I place my hand over hers on the table and look into her brown eyes. She looks so tired. The lines on her face crinkle as she forces a smile, then she places a kiss on the back of my hand.

PART 2
THE DARK
PLACE

In the back of the transport van.
Rumbling road.
Rumbling tyres.
Darkness
For hours.
Sweaty, hot.
We stop.
The back door opens.
White light rushing in.
A man's hand on me.
A handful of my shirt.
He pulls me out.
Handcuffs on my wrists
Click into place.
The sunlight is blinding.
The white fades.
Big building ahead
With tall walls.

Barbed wire lines the tops of them.

A sign on the wall: *Kinston Juvenile Justice Centre.*

A hand on my shoulder.

A shove.

Walking, legs still waking up.

Into an opened garage.

Roller door lowers when I'm inside.

A silver door ahead.

Swipe card on black pad.

Bzzzzzzz.

Door clicks open.

Carpet floor.

Air is cooler.

White walls.

Framed pictures – newspaper clippings.

Photographs of kids from the eighties, nineties.

Heart is thumping.

I can feel it beating in my throat.

Palms sweating, wet on my neck.

A bad place.

A dark place.

Swipe card on black pad.

Bzzzzzzz.

Door clicks open.

Tall woman –

The tallest I've ever seen.

Big muscles.

Tattoos.

Name tag: *Maggie.*

'How much do you bench, miss?' I ask.

'More than you,' she replies.

Cuffs are unlocked. Blood returning to my hands.

Maggie holds a paper.

She reads.

Blah. Blah. Blah.

She walks me to the corner of the room to change.

A curtain is my only privacy.

She hands me

Folded clothes, still warm.

A pair of crappy cheap-looking shoes.

Size ten.

They replace my real shoes: black Nikes.

These cheap slip-ons don't even have laces

For fuck's sake.

A shoe isn't really a shoe if it has no laces.

Curtain across.

I undress to my underwear.

Pull on black shorts.

Pull on white polo shirt

Which belonged to someone else.

Slide the crappy shoes onto my feet.

No cushioning in the soles.

A mirror.

Me in the mirror.

I don't want to look, because

A bad kid stares back.

A kid who is me, but I don't know him.

My own stuff collected by Maggie.

'This will go into your *property*.'

Two juvie screws come into the room.

They're tall and muscly too.

Wearing armour.

Padding around their torsos

And shoulders

And thighs.

Big boots.

Batons on their waist.

Big men.

Bulletproof.

Little, skinny, harmless me.

'These fellas will take you to the Induction Unit, where you'll settle in,' Maggie says.

A new screw enters – tall man

With black eyes,

A crew cut and a name tag: *Alex*.

'Hands in front,' Alex says. 'I'm one of the Unit supervisors. We're in charge here. Got it?'

I nod.

New handcuffs slap on my wrists.

Sounds like a ticking clock as they tighten around my bones.

'That hurts,' I say.

'Don't be a pussy,' Alex says. 'You've ended up in here. You're not a good person, so don't expect to be treated like one.'

Alex towers over me, takes a strong hold of my bicep.

Into another corridor.

Alex and the two kitted screws escorting me.

White walls.

Smell of chicken noodles.

Swipe card on black pad.

Bzzzzzzz.

Door clicks open.

Outside, between buildings.

Buildings all around me like giants.

Sun shines over the tops of them.

Fresh air.

A pathway.

Sand and rocks.

Garden.

Flowers and native plants and benches and tables.

Smells like laundry powder.

At the end of the pathway stands a big steel-barred door.

Metal key clicks into the lock.

Big steel-barred door opens.

Inside.

A tall door on a tall wall.

Swipe card on black pad.

Bzzzzzzz.

Door clicks open.

More swipes.

More black pads.

More *bzzzzzzz.*

Doors click open.

Metal key into the lock.

A steel-barred door opens.

Back outside.

Fresh air again.

Footpath around a big square court.

Concrete ground.

A basketball hoop standing at one end.

Screw in front of me.

Alex and screw behind me.

Small office-looking building.

Door opens.

Cool air inside.

Looks like the front office at school.

A man with a red beard in a black shirt.

Another boy wearing a white polo shirt.

He's African.

Glances at me when I walk in.

TV on the wall.

Ellen DeGeneres's show is playing.

'I'm Greg, the Induction Unit manager,' the man at the counter says. 'Follow me.'

I follow Greg, Greg in front.

Look over my shoulder.

Alex's black eyes watch me

Walk into the hallway.

Greg opens a door.

Small room.

My room.

A toilet.

A shower.

A single bed.

A big fluffy-looking pillow.

'You'll soon move into one of the units with the other detainees,' Greg says.

I look to the pillow.

I'm exhausted.

Tired.

Want to lie down

But not yet.

Hallway.

Common area.

Outside to courtyard.

Phone.

Dial Aunty Dawn's number.

Ring, ring.

Ring, ring.

Ring, ring.

BEEP.

|||

'You are receiving a call from Kinston Juvenile Justice Centre. If you wish to accept this call, please stay on the line. If you don't wish to accept this call, please hang up now.'

Silence.

Rustle.

'Hello?'

'Jamie? That you?' Uncle Bobby answers.

'Yeah, it's me, Unk. I'm at Kinston. I'm in the Induction Unit. I think it's like an orientation or something. But I'm okay. I just wanted to let youse know.'

'No worries, Jamie. Keep your head up, yeah? Hopefully you'll be out of there in a month after you go to court, so you won't have to wait too long.'

'Yeah, hopefully,' I say, resting against the wall.

'Aunt's just at the shops at the moment. She was gonna stop in at Family Services to have a yarn with your caseworker, but I'll let her know you called. You know how she is, always forgetting to take her phone with her.' Uncle Bobby yawns.

'I'm sorry, Unk,' I say. 'I'm sorry about all this.'

He's quiet for a moment.

'I know, son. Just hang in there, all right?'

'Yeah, Unk.'

III

My shoes tap on the concrete floor.

Common area.

Hallway.

Room.

Fluffy pillow.

Dark.

Peace.

Calm.

Quiet.

Light.

Nothing.

Nothing.

Nothing.

III

A knock at my door.

Woman standing there.

She doesn't look like a screw.

A short girl with brown hair.

She wears a black lanyard and her shirt is different to the other screws'. It's got a goanna across the front in the style of an Aboriginal dot painting. She's Koori.

'Jamie Langton, yeah?' the Koori girl asks, opening the door. 'Mind if I come in for a sec?'

'Sure.'

Koori girl looks young.

Maybe a few years older than me.

Her eyes scan the room.

'I'm Shae. I'm one of the Aboriginal youth workers here,' she says. 'How are you settling in?'

'Not bad, I guess. A double bed would be better,' I say.

Shae smiles. 'Well, this isn't exactly a luxurious resort, is it?'

I shrug my shoulders.

I'm pretty keen for her to go away so I can sleep.

'I'm here to help,' she says. 'Anything you need, or if you have any issues, or even if you're just feeling no good, you can come to me. We do a lot of programs in here for the Koori boys, so when you go along to those, I'll probably be there.'

'Are there many other Kooris in here?'

'A few,' Shae replies. 'More than I would like there to be.'

I rest back on the pillow, hoping that Shae will take the hint to go away.

'I'll see you again soon, Jamie. Keep your head up.'

Keep your head up: the phrase of the day.

Shae gives me a little smile – a real smile – then she's gone.

Roof is white.

Sigh.

My new home.

Night comes.

Shouting comes too.

Ruckus in the nearby units.

'I'll see ya tomorrow, Benji,' someone shouts. 'You're dead tomorrow—'

'Shut up! I'm trying to fucking sleep!' someone else shouts.

'Come at me, bruh! I'll break your jaw!'

Someone's just screaming and hollering.

Someone's howling.

Someone's banging something against metal.

'Get to sleep! Now!' an adult shouts. 'Cut it out!'

Noise doesn't stop.

Noise remains.

My palms sweat.

Heart racing.

Chest rocketing.

Faster and faster.

Noise.

Wild noise.

Chaotic.

My stay here at Kinston won't be a walk in the park.

The fear boils in my stomach.

Mark Cassidy and the lads might not get the chance to kill me after all.

I
Might
Die
In
Here.

III

Next day.

Breakfast.

Soggy cornflakes.

Spoon dings the bowl with each scoop.

I sip the milk.

Milk spills down my chin

To my chest.

I wipe it up with my shirt.

Greg comes in.

Screw behind him.

She's carrying a red polo shirt in her hand.

Folded.

Big smile.

Walkie-talkie on her belt.

Wire goes all the way up to an earpiece.

'Hey, Jamie. How are you going?'

'I miss drinking Coke.'

Giggles.

'. . . moving you to the Red Unit now.'

Three weeks until court.

I just need to tough it out.

Swipe card on black pad.

Bzzzzzzz.

Door clicks open.

'Why do the boys make so much noise at night?' I ask. 'Do they do that every night?'

'Not *every* night. Some of them just like to disturb the peace,' screw says.

Swipe card on black pad.

Bzzzzzzz.

Door clicks open.

Cement path

Between the cut grass.

Little plants grow in places along the way.

Two screws accompany us.

No handcuffs.

Swipe card on black pad.

Bzzzzzzz.

Door clicks open.

Small building.

Futuristic demountable classroom.

All boys sitting around a table

Eating cornflakes.

Fifteen of them.

Mostly black faces.

A few white kids.

An Asian guy.

All eyes on me.

Don't know what to do.

Little nod.

I follow the screw.

Hallway looks like a hospital dorm.

White walls.

Boards at the side of each door.

Keys jingle.

She unlocks a room.

Room number four.

My room.

Same as the last

But this room has a TV mounted on the wall.

She hands me my red polo shirt.

I take off the white, put on the red.

Dusty room.

Dust finds my nostrils.

Sneeze.

Little window.

She slides it open.

'The boys are still having brekky,' she says. 'Why don't you come out and introduce yourself.'

Back to the common room.

'I'll come check on you tomorrow.'

She leaves the unit.

Seat is hard on my arse.

Boy beside me's a Koori boy.

Biggest mole on his cheek.

'Where you from, cuz?' mole-boy asks.

'Dalton's Bay.'

'Jamie?' someone asks.

Another black face across the table.

He's familiar.

'Remember me?' he asks.

And just like that, I do.

Ryan Smith.

Skinny Koori boy.

Arms like noodles.

Bony fists.

Lived in Dalton's Bay.

Went to my school

A few years ago.

Class clown.

Always laughing.

III

I remember Ryan told me at the time that his family was moving around a fair bit, so I wasn't surprised when he suddenly stopped coming to school and I never saw him again.

'Ryan?' I ask. 'What are you doing in 'ere?'

'I stabbed this lad when I was off my head,' he says.

'Why'd you do that?' I ask.

'We just had a fight and I stabbed him. I was off my chops. Wasn't really thinking.'

'That's no good, cuz,' I say.

'Yeah. Been here about seven months now. Or eight. No, seven, I think. But I get out in a couple weeks, so it's all good. What you in for?' Ryan asks.

'Stole a car.' I hear myself saying it. Why the fuck did we steal Mark Cassidy's car? So stupid. 'Might be here for a while. I dunno.'

'Yeah, true. This lad's Kevin,' he says, pointing to mole-boy.

I shake Kevin's hand. 'Nice to meet ya.'

Through the glass doors of the unit we can hear yelling in the courtyard. One of the boys is shouting through the fence to another Aboriginal boy who's walking with a screw outside the gate. He's wearing a purple polo shirt and has messy curly hair. I can't tell what they're saying, but it sounds like the boy outside the unit is going off.

'Who's that in the purple?' I ask.

'That's Ronnie,' Ryan says. 'He's in the Purple Unit. Don't get on his bad side. He's high classo. Been in and out of here for years.'

Ronnie.

Stubble on his chin.

Misshapen nose.

Thick eyebrows.

Big, strong arms.

I couldn't take him in a fight.

A screw comes in through the glass doors, keys and cards jingling at his waist.

'Jamie Langton?' he asks.

I put up my hand.

'You got a visit,' he says.

'A visit?'

'Yeah, come on. I'll take you up to the visit area.'

Aunty Dawn's come to see me. Maybe Uncle Bobby came with her.

'Is it my Aunty Dawn?'

'Aunty? Nah, some Aboriginal fella. I think his name was *Trent* or *Trey*.'

'Trey? My brother?'

'If an Aboriginal fella named Trey is your brother, then I'd say so. Now come on, I don't have all day.'

Trey has come to visit.

The radio was on in Uncle Bobby's car, but as we arrived home from school, the yelling from the house was so loud it drowned out the song that was playing through the speakers.

After we parked, Uncle Bobby sighed. 'Come on,' he said.

When I got out of the car, I realised it was Trey's voice that was yelling. There was banging and the glass windows were shaking as I followed Uncle Bobby up the stairs and inside.

'Trey, you have to stop now,' Aunty Dawn shouted.

'Fuck you! You don't know what it's like for me. You don't know!' Trey shouted. His bedroom door was closed, and Aunty Dawn was standing at it with tears all over her face. There was another bang and Trey screamed inside.

'Best go to your room, son,' Uncle Bobby said. I went to my room and closed the door. I could hear Trey crying through the wall. Then another bang shocked me. I dropped my schoolbag to the floor and got in my bed, pulled the blanket over myself.

'You can't just take off,' Aunty Dawn shouted.

'Yes, I can,' Trey shouted back. 'I'm sixteen. You can't control me anymore! You wanna bury me next week? I'll stay if that's what you wanna do!'

I took a deep breath. My heart was beating so fast. I tried to think of the song that was playing in the car on the radio. I liked it, but I didn't know what it was called, so I tried to remember the lyrics and replay them in my head.

I heard Trey's door open with a bang against the wall.

'Let's talk about this. Please, Trey?' Aunty Dawn pleaded.

'Get out of my way, Aunt,' Trey shouted back. 'Move!'

'Trey, calm down,' Aunty Dawn said.

'Get out of the way, Dawn,' Uncle Bobby said. 'Let 'im go.'

'No! I'm not gonna stand here and watch him disappear,' Aunty Dawn shouted.

'You know where I'm going,' Trey shouted back. 'Just move!'

'Trey,' Aunty Dawn said.

'Move! Move! Move! Move! Please just fucking move! Get out of my way!' Trey shouted, louder. It sounded like his throat was tearing to pieces. Aunty Dawn began to cry. Footsteps boomed on the ground. They grew further away and the shouting began again, but it was quieter. They were outside.

I pushed the blanket away, got out of bed. I walked to my door and creeped it open. I could see Aunty Dawn crying on the verandah and Uncle Bobby had his arms around her.

I stepped into the hallway. One of the hinges was broken on Trey's door and it was wonky. In Trey's room there were papers, socks, underwear and pieces of plaster from the wall all over the floor. The walls were covered in holes. All of Trey's cupboards were opened and emptied. It looked like a hurricane had blasted through. I didn't understand. Had he just run away? Where had he gone?

I rushed out to the verandah as my eyes began to sting with tears, but Trey wasn't there, just Aunty Dawn and Uncle Bobby.

9

Swipe card on black pad.
Bzzzzzz.
Door clicks open.
Leaving the unit.
Courtyard.
Grassy area.
Sweat along my spine.
No handcuffs.
Along the footpath.
My shoes are squeaky.
Swipe card on black pad.
Bzzzzzz.
Door clicks open.
Laundry-powder-smelling garden.
Swipe card on black pad.
Bzzzzzz.
Door clicks open.
ADMINISTRATION.

Airconditioner is soothing.

Arrow on the wall

Says: *VISIT AREA.*

Long corridor.

Screw walking ahead of me.

Swipe card on black pad.

Bzzzzzzz.

Door clicks open.

No airconditioner in this corridor.

Heat trapped in here.

Pictures on the wall.

Kinston's front office

In 1988.

Black and white.

Swipe card on black pad.

Bzzzzzzz.

Door clicks open.

Reception area.

Cubicles.

'Here, Langton,' screw says.

New corridor.

Glass doors.

Visit rooms.

BOX ROOMS.

A glass window separating *DETAINEE* from *VISITOR.*

Empty.

Empty.

Black boy I haven't seen yet.

Green polo,

His back to me,

Talking to some white woman in a suit pencilling something into her notepad.

CONTACT ROOMS.

No glass window.

A little table at the centre.

We arrive to the contact room at the end of the corridor and there he is: Trey.

III

Trey's really here.

He's older.

Must be like twenty-two now, I think.

His cheeks are bigger, covered in short facial hair.

He's got a beer belly.

He's wearing a black polo shirt with the Aboriginal and Torres Strait Islander flags patched across his heart.

He's got short black hair, which consists of a curly bundle on top and a faded short-cut around the sides.

I study him as the screw unlocks the door with his big metal key. Trey stands when I walk in and the screws lock the door behind me. There is a blue chair on my side of the table. Trey extends his hand over to me and we shake hands. He sits down in his chair and I sit down in mine.

'Aunty Dawn called me. Said you were in 'ere,' Trey says.

'Mmm.'

Trey sits back, folds his arms. 'Are you gonna tell me what happened, or what?'

'Was just bein' stupid,' I say, letting my arms dangle on either side of the chair as I rest back.

'Being stupid?' he asks, sitting back with a sigh.

'Why do you care?' I ask. Trey doesn't answer. 'We were just getting back at the lads. They walk around like they own the place, fuck with us whenever they want. They had it comin'. The only thing I feel bad about is that we got caught.'

'Come on, Jamie,' Trey says, rolling his eyes. 'I know you're smarter than this. You were always curious about everything, always asking questions. How could you let yourself end up in here?'

'I didn't just *let myself*,' I say. 'It was Dally and Lenny too. We did it together. We didn't think it through.'

'You can't blame your mates for your decisions. You could've chosen not to get in that car.'

'Who are you to tell me what I could and couldn't choose to do? I haven't seen you in years. You left me. You don't even know me.'

'I'm your brother, you idiot. I know you better than anyone.'

It falls quiet between us. Even though I'm annoyed, I've kind of missed him being my protective big brother.

'No matter what, I'll just end up back in juvie,' I say. 'I know I will.'

'You don't have to,' he says, leaning forward. 'You can be better. You can go another way.'

'Okay, you're starting to sound like a wizard.'

'It's up to you, Jamie,' he says. 'I know it's probably hard to see right now, but you can do better. All you have to do is try.'

I want to talk back, tell him he's living in some fantasy world, but I won't.

'So, what's new with you?' I ask. I rest my foot up on the table to push myself back a little, balancing on the back legs of the chair. 'Where you livin' now?'

'Sydney, still. I work for a youth program in the Western Suburbs,' Trey says. 'Been there for about a year now.'

'A youth program? What kind of stuff do you do?'

'Umm, sports mostly. It's all about healthy living, healthy choices. We did our first camp a couple months ago. Took some of the Koori boys out on country for a night.'

'Oh yeah? There's this brother named Travis who runs camps back home. I went on one just before I got locked up, but I fucking hate camping. He works at the youth centre in DB.'

Trey chuckles. 'Yeah, I went to school with Travis. I remember Aunty Dawn and Uncle Bobby took us camping one Christmas and you were going on the whole time about the mozzies. They liked your blood, for some reason.'

'Well, who wouldn't be worried about mozzies?' I say. 'They carry diseases, don't they?'

Trey laughs and his cheeks flush with red. I crack up too, and suddenly it feels like it's the first time I've laughed in years, like we're little kids again.

'I've got a partner now,' Trey says when we calm down. 'His name is Jacob. He's at uni, studying to be a lawyer. We've been together for a year and a half.'

'A year and a half? How could anyone put up with ya for that long?'

We both burst into laughter again and we don't stop until my ribs are sore and my eyes are getting wet.

'You know I had to leave, right?' Trey says. 'I had to get out of Dalton's Bay, you know? I had to do it for *me*. It wasn't because of you or anything. It wasn't because of Aunty Dawn or Uncle Bobby. It was all about me. Maybe it was even a little selfish. I dunno.'

I just nod. 'Yeah, I know. All good.'

'It was a bit nerve-racking, coming in 'ere. I had to put all my stuff in a locker, come through one of those security scanner things, then through three locked doors.'

I chuckle again. 'Yeah, it's a shitty place.'

'Are there many Koori boys in there with ya?'

'Yeah. Most of the boys in my unit are Aboriginal, I think.' I stand for a moment to crack my back. 'You still go for the Panthers?'

'Yep,' Trey says. 'I've been to a couple home games. You still going for the Cowboys?'

'Yeah, even though Thurston's retired now. Gotta stick with 'em.'

'I remember when you got that headgear that looked like Thurston's,' Trey says. 'You wore it for two years straight until your head got too big for it. Are you still playing footy?'

'Nah,' I say. 'I stopped after fourteens.'

'Why?'

'The lads. They're all arseholes. They started doggin' me and my mates, and they reckon they're all better than us. Guess it don't matter now.'

'Well,' he says, in that tone where I know he's about to try to teach me a lesson, 'you know you could do some exercise while you're in here? Get yourself fit again for when you get out.'

I laugh. 'I cooouuulllddd.'

Trey sits forward again.

'Did Mum and Dad call you?' he asks.

'Mum called Aunty Dawn. I didn't talk to 'em.'

'I'm gonna go see them, see Dad. If you're in here for a while, I could bring them in.'

'No,' I say. 'I don't wanna see them. Especially not in here.'

'I know it probably makes you feel like shit, thinking about Mum and Dad. You probably reckon our lives turned out the way they did because of them. You might even feel a bit angry or something, and that would be all right too.'

'I'm not angry,' I say. 'I don't care. It is what it is.'

He nods and brushes the non-existent beard on his clean-shaven chin.

Trey has changed. He's different. He's not that same boy who was punching holes in his walls that day – the boy who had a screaming match with Aunty Dawn. He's not the same boy who stormed out and didn't look back.

10

Back in the unit, I head straight across the courtyard. This bearded lad who smells like three days' worth of sweat is on the phone.

'How long you gonna be?' I ask. He doesn't respond. 'I need to make a call.'

'Fuck off,' stinky bearded boy snaps over his shoulder, covering the phone with his hand. I turn away. I don't want to get in a fight with this guy, because I'll be showering for days if he touches me.

I look towards the unit, but I can't see Ryan inside. He's not in the courtyard, either.

I walk back to the centre of the courtyard, where one of the boys is about to try for a three-pointer at the basketball hoop.

He lands the shot and rushes after the ball. He throws it back to me and I dribble the ball at the three-pointer line. I glance over to stinky bearded boy and he's still on the phone.

I shoot my shot and miss the hoop completely. The boy dribbles back and lands another perfect three-pointer.

'Five minutes until lunch,' one of the screws shouts from the unit.

I head back to the phone and stinky bearded boy is still talking flat out.

'You're not listening to me,' he says to the person on the phone. He's in an argument. He's fired up. If I try to get him off the phone, he'll attack me.

I turn away and then I see Shae coming out of the unit. She waves me over.

'Jamie,' she says. 'We've got an Aboriginal dance program starting this Friday. Would you be interested in doing that? Most of the boys have put their names down.'

'Nah, that's okay. I'm not much of a dancer.'

'What if you just came along for a look?' she asks.

'I don't wanna. Thanks, though.'

'Okay. Well, I'll check in with you again soon. I know this isn't the best place in the world to be, so if you need to talk or anything, just let me know. I'm here most days,' she says, then she heads for the gate and lets herself out of the unit.

I think Shae is pretty nice. I might even like her, but I reckon she's one of those adults that really desperately wants to help us kids, but not because we need it, because it makes them feel better to think they might be helping us.

'Lunch is served,' the screw says. 'Inside now, boys.'

Stinky bearded boy finally gets off the phone and starts for the unit. I just want to call Aunty Dawn, but I head inside to the table along with the other boys. The screws hand us plates of chicken schnitzel and microwaved mixed vegetables.

'Where's Ryan?' I ask Kevin, taking a seat beside him.

'He had a bit of an episode this morning,' Kevin says.

'An episode?'

'Yeah. He's got problems.'

I shove some of the chicken schnitzel into my mouth. It's chewy and wet, cold in the middle. I spit it back out and notice Kevin doing the same. He's got a freshly black eye. A cut is still open below his bottom eyelid.

'What happened to you?' I ask.

'Ronnie,' Kevin says. 'We were doing that coffee-making program in the morning and he whacked me.'

'Why?'

'He said I was putting too much coffee in the grinder-thing. I told him it was a good amount.'

'So, he hit you over *coffee*?'

'Yeah, he's a prick,' Kevin says. 'He's been in and out of lock-up since he was eleven. Don't start any shit with him and you'll be right.'

I think about that all through dinner and then again when I'm back in my room. Kevin's a good guy. He wouldn't start a fight for no reason. This Ronnie's just a dickhead. I haven't even talked to him or anything, and I already hate him.

After lunch, a screw, a younger girl, enters the unit with a guy in a green shirt and sporty shorts. His shoes are flash runners, shining red.

'We've got an afternoon footy program for the Aboriginal boys. If you want to come, line up,' she says. The footy guy is tall and fit. His calves look like rocks on the backs of his legs.

I join the few boys who line up at the gates. Two screws lead us outside and we follow the pathway past all the other units, until we have ten Aboriginal boys. We walk in pairs through the gates with one of the screws at the front of our line and one at the back. A couple of the boys say a few things to each other and the screw at the front turns back to them.

'Oi. No talking during movements.'

The boys stay quiet until the screws take us through the gate and onto the oval. The footy guy in the green jersey is setting up fluoro cones to make a square across the middle of the oval.

On his way back to us, he passes the football to Kevin.

'I'm Darren,' he says. 'I'm here for your rugby league program this arvo.'

A few of the boys whisper to each other. My thoughts are dominated by the heat raging down on us from the cloudless sky.

'So, we'll play a game of touch a bit later, but I wanted to have a chat with you guys about healthy living,' Darren says. 'Do any of you use the gym equipment here?'

Half of the boys raise their hands.

'Well, it's important to keep active, even if you're in a place where you can't do much, right?' Darren continues while a couple of boys behind me whisper something and then burst out laughing. 'You can do things like push-ups and sit-ups in your rooms.'

It's warm out here on the oval and sweaty patches have quickly gathered at my armpits. There aren't any tall trees to shade us, so we're under the sun.

'Do we want to play some games to warm up?' Darren asks. 'Or do we want to jump into a game of touch?'

'Touch,' Kevin and a boy with braces say at the same time.

Kevin and the boy with braces are made captains and Kevin chooses me first. We begin the game and I kick off. I'm sweating after just a few metres of jogging.

'Tip the criminal...'

'Stop being a hog and pass the ball, ya fat fuck...'

'Run faster! Pretend the coppers are chasin' ya...'

I'm so slow today that I can't get a touch on anyone. Kevin is a fucking sprinter. He could be in the Olympics, I reckon. He's way faster than me.

At the end of the game, Kevin has scored four tries and single-handedly beaten us. My team only managed two tries. I'm practically collapsing on the grass when the rugby league guy calls for drinks break. I'm so unfit it isn't funny.

After the program, the two screws walk us back to our units. 'You've got ten minutes until lockdown,' the girl screw says, as she drops off me and Kevin and the other boys from my unit.

She locks the gate behind us and we walk across the courtyard. As I head to the unit, Ryan comes outside from the common area. My heart races at the sight of him.

'Brother, I missed ya,' I say. I sit opposite him.

'Next time I go, I'll give ya a picture of me so you can put it on your wall and look at it when you miss me,' Ryan says. I just laugh and he laughs too. I feel at ease seeing him, knowing he's all right, and I can't help but stare at the bandages on his arms, from his thumbs right up to his elbows.

He picks up a basketball and dribbles back a few metres. He bounces the ball in front of his feet a few times, then shoots. The ball deflects off the metal hoop and I leap to catch it. I jog back, dribbling the ball on my way to where Ryan is. He nurses his left arm, scratching lightly on the bandage.

'Stitches?' I ask.

'Yeah, they're itchy as fuck right now.'

'What did you do?' I ask, thinking maybe if I sound oblivious, he'll make up some lie and I'll decide to believe it, because even though I want to understand, it's a bit of an awkward conversation.

'Cut myself,' he says.

I bounce the ball a couple of times, then shoot. It falls into the hoop without a sound.

'Were you trying to kill yourself?'

'No,' Ryan says. He's got a weird little smirk on his face and his cheeks are turning red.

'Then why would you cut yourself?'

'I dunno. I was sad.'

'You were sad, so you cut up your arms?'

Ryan walks to get the basketball. I follow him for a few steps, then let him go ahead.

'I don't know,' he says, his voice quietening to almost a whisper. 'I guess I just wanted to feel something else.'

He passes the basketball to me and I hold it against my stomach. I take another shot and the ball bounces off the hoop and back towards me.

'Are you all right now, though?' I ask. Ryan shrugs. 'I mean, you're not gonna do it again, are you?'

He just shrugs again.

'Five minutes until lockdown,' one of the screws shouts from the unit.

I rush to the phone. Alex, the tall, fit screw with the crew cut and black eyes, spots me and walks towards the entrance of the unit. He leans against the side of the door and watches me. He's chewing gum. He tilts his head back and looks down at me over his chin.

I turn away, dial Aunty Dawn's number. The phone beeps after one ring and the automated message plays.

'Aunt?'

'Jamie,' she says. Her voice rests over my ear like a pillow and it's the best, most beautiful sound in the world.

'How are you?' I ask. Aunty Dawn starts giggling. 'Why you laughin'?'

'You've never asked me how I am before,' she says.

'Really? Nah, I ask you all the time. I'm sure.'

'You don't,' Aunty Dawn says. 'But I'm good, son. I've been taking calls and just hung up the phone thirty seconds before you rang. Trey let me know he's been to visit you.'

'Yeah, he spun me out. He was the last person I thought I'd see.'

Aunty Dawn giggles again. Her giggle makes me smile. It makes me forget for a moment that I'm stuck behind these walls.

'How are you coping?' Aunty Dawn asks. 'You lookin' after yourself? Keepin' outta trouble? Not getting into any fights, I hope.'

'Nah, no fights. It's pretty laid back in 'ere, actually,' I say, resting against the wall.

'Good, good. You only got a couple weeks till court. Keep your head up until then, okay?'

'Yeah,' I say.

'I love you, Jamie-baby,' Aunty Dawn says. My cheeks are instantly hot and I'm sure I'm blushing. I've never told her I love her. That kind of thing isn't really *us*.

'Love ya too, Aunt,' I say. 'I'll call you again before court.'

'Okay, son. Talk then.'

I hang up, head back to the unit. Alex has his arms folded across his chest as I pass him. I can feel his black eyes staring right into my soul.

At bedtime, I head to my room and close the door behind me. I'm wide awake, though. I lie on my back and stare at the ceiling. I wonder what Dally and Lenny are doing right now. I wonder if they're also on their backs, staring at the ceiling wondering how the fuck this happened.

Footsteps click on the ground. It must be like ten o'clock when I look to the small square window on my door. The shadow casts against the wall outside, then a figure steps into the frame.

It's Alex. His face is silhouetted, but it's him. He's stopped there, staring in at me through the window. There's no smile, no frown, just blankness. He's going to open the door and walk into my room. He wants to hurt me. He wants to kill me.

Alex's shadowy face moves away from my window and my heart is pounding. I can hear my own breaths so loudly it's like they are bouncing off the concrete walls. Then his footsteps click on the ground again. They grow distant as he walks away.

I sigh when I hear a door open and close. I pull the blanket over my head and hide myself. This is a bad place. Bad things happen here. This is no place to call home.

I find myself thinking about Aunty Dawn. I remember when me and Trey first moved to her place. I asked her when I was going back to live with Mum and Dad and she said I wasn't. She said her home was my home now. We sat in a room and she asked me what I could change to make that room my own. I said 'a poster of the Cowboys', so she ordered a poster of Johnathan Thurston which I Blu-Tacked to the wall. She helped me make her house my home. I wish she was in here with me. No matter how hard I try to forget that I'm in a cage, this place doesn't feel like home.

We removed our new Hot Wheels cars from their packets and took them to the backyard. Trey dug into the dirt and grass to make a little road for our cars, which zigged and zagged along the edge of the garden before crossing the bridge he'd made from an old broken fence paling and set down among the flowers and weeds.

Something was lingering on my mind. Trey was older and always seemed to have the answers to any question I had.

'Trey,' I said, as he was digging a slope for our cars in the dirt. 'Trey?'

'What?' he asked, sounding annoyed.

'Why do we have brown skin but other kids have white skin?'

'We have brown skin because we're Aboriginal,' he said. 'White people have white skin because they're white.'

'But why are they white?'

'Their ancestors came from England and other places in Europe – where their white skin comes from. Our ancestors were always in Australia – where our brown skin comes from.'

I looked to Aunty Dawn and Uncle Bobby through the glass doors. They were in the kitchen preparing dinner together, Archie Roach blasting from the speakers.

'Why aren't we allowed to live with Mum and Dad anymore?' I asked Trey.

'Because the white people think they're bad parents,' Trey said.

'But why do the white people get to choose who the bad parents are and who the good parents are?'

'I don't know. Why you asking?'

'One of my friends at school wanted to know why I don't live with my parents anymore.'

'Tell them that's none of their business,' Trey said.

I stood up and guided my red speedster across the bridge, imagined it zooming through a jungle with branches and vines threatening to obstruct it. I performed a handbrake spin on the bridge and caught a splinter in my finger. I was about to start crying when Trey grabbed my hand.

'Be more careful,' Trey said, as he dug the splinter from my skin with his fingernails.

11

Morning.
Cornflakes for breakfast.
Rec time sitting in the common area
Watching TV.
School
Even in here.
Maths class.
English.
Ham sandwiches for lunch.
School.
Art class.
Afternoon program.
Rec time.
Phone call to Aunty Dawn.
Lockdown.
Chicken schnitzel for dinner.
Lockdown.
Nighttime.

Dark room, dark walls.

Morning.

Cornflakes for breakfast.

Rec time sitting in the common area

Watching TV.

School.

Chicken wraps for lunch.

School.

Afternoon program.

Rec time.

Phone call to Aunty Dawn.

No answer, leave voicemail.

Lockdown.

Turkey rissoles for dinner.

Lockdown.

Nighttime.

Dark room, dark walls.

Morning.

Cornflakes for breakfast.

Rec time sitting in the common area

Watching TV.

School.

Fish fingers for lunch.

School.

Afternoon program.

Rec time.

Phone call to Aunty Dawn.

Uncle Bobby answers.

Lockdown.

Sausages and mash for dinner.

Lockdown.

Nighttime.

Dark room, dark walls.

The same

Every day.

Cycle repeats.

Same room.

Same walls.

Hours.

Days.

Weeks.

III

Three weeks have breezed by in Kinston Juvenile Holiday Resort. I wait with Ryan outside the visit area. The screw is talking on their radio – something about their black swipe card not working.

'I'm getting out next week,' Ryan says. 'Had a chat with my legal aid. Five days left for me.'

'That's good, cuz,' I say. 'You'll get to go home where those workers cook ya food and drive ya round.'

'Yeah,' he says quietly, and it seems like his mouth can hardly get the word out.

'Aren't ya happy?'

'Yeah, I'm happy,' he says. 'I'll just miss all the boys in 'ere. I know I'll just get stuck in the same shit when I get out. Maybe I'll even want to come back.'

'No,' I say. It's laughable. 'You don't wanna come back in here, cuz.'

'Why not? It's just…I dunno. I'm gonna get pissed when I get out. So I got that to look forward to.'

'Hey,' I say, 'do you know that screw named Alex? Is he like a psycho or something? He was staring at me through my window the other night.'

'He's just a dog,' Ryan replies. 'You gotta pay no attention to the shit he says and does.'

The black swipe card finally works and the screw takes us into the visit area. The screw lets Ryan into one of the non-contact rooms and locks me into the one beside it. Trey is sitting patiently on the other side of the glass, though his hair is a mess and he has bags under his eyes.

'You just roll out of bed?' I ask. He chuckles and shakes his head as I take a seat on the stool they've given me. I rest my elbows on the metal desk. Between us is a thick sheet of glass.

'Only had a few hours sleep,' Trey says. 'I had to go to the police station last night for a client.'

'Oh. What happened?'

Trey rubs his eyes; they are bloodshot.

'He was just a bit drunk and got into a fight with someone. They called the cops and he got arrested. He got bail at six a.m. So, I went home and had a shower, then drove out here.'

I laugh. 'You shoulda just cancelled and had a sleep-in.'

'Nah,' Trey says, straightening his back. 'I don't cancel on my brother. I grabbed a coffee on the way, so I should be right for the visit at least.'

I don't cancel on my brother – says the guy who didn't bother to see me for three years.

'Court's only a few days away. Excited?' Trey asks.

'Nah,' I say. 'I'll just be sitting there for hours in the video room and then they'll talk in their legal bullshit language and tell me I ain't getting bail again.'

'You never know,' he says. 'Do they have any Aboriginal programs for you in here?'

'Yeah, there was this dancing one, but I didn't want to do it.'

Trey nods. 'You never know, you might like it.'

'I might like *dancing*? I think not.' I chuckle. 'The boys reckon another program's starting soon. Teaching us about culture and stuff.'

'It's not *just* dancing,' Trey says. 'It's telling stories, like our ancestors did. It's feeling their strength as you tell the stories, tapping into our culture, which has survived for thousands and thousands of years.'

'Calm down,' I say, forcing myself to hold in my laughter.

'You shouldn't be afraid or ashamed of dancing in the traditional way or of learning about our culture. The government tried to take all that away, kill off our culture, but because of the old people who came before us, it's still alive. You get to continue our culture when you dance. It's in your blood.'

'All right,' I say as I sit back in my seat. It really does feel nice to have Trey come and visit me. To see him, to talk to him again.

'You were a big dancer when you were little,' Trey teases.

'Fuck off.'

'You were! You'd watch The Wiggles on TV in the afternoons. You'd be up dancing along with them and Mum would record you on her phone.'

'Oh, did she?'

'Yeah. Her camera was shit, though. I wonder if she's still got those videos. I thought it was annoying then, but now those are some of my happiest memories of living with Mum and Dad: watching you dancing to The Wiggles while Mum recorded ya, smiling from ear to ear.'

'Buulllllshiiiiiiiiiiiiiit,' I say, folding my arms. I can't help but feel Trey is living in some fantasy world in his head. He reckons those days were happy, but they can't have been.

The visit ends and I'm taken back to my room. I've barely got my arse on my bed when there's a knock at the door.

'Hey, mate. Mind if I come in?' It's Shae, the Koori youth worker.

'Umm, yeah, sure,' I say, sitting up as she walks into my room carrying a small cardboard box.

'How are ya goin'?' Shae asks.

'All good,' I say.

'I was wondering if I could get you to help me out with something?' she says. 'It's a surprise.'

'What? That sounds shady,' I say.

'Don't worry. It's not a dance program or anything. Ryan's coming along too.'

I wipe some sweat from my forehead and stand. 'Okay, fine.'

I join Ryan at the unit gate and Shae and another screw take us out, reminding us not to talk during the movement. The warmth from the air feels like there are heaters surrounding my body, and the sweat comes back to my forehead.

It's only a few minutes to the other end of the courtyard, but it feels like I've walked a marathon by the time we make it to a white building block. Shae walks ahead of us and while she unlocks the door, I get a peek inside the window. It looks like a classroom in there.

It's even warmer when I follow Shae inside – like the heat has been trapped. There are shelves on every wall that are stacked with books.

'This is the library,' Shae says. The other screw crosses the room to turn the aircon on. Me and Ryan rush to stand in the blast of cool air.

'Jesus,' Ryan says. 'That's lovely.'

'Come over here,' Shae says.

'What do you need our help with?' I ask, walking back to where she's standing by the bookshelf. I'm just tired now – the cool air is too relaxing after being so drained by the heat.

'I'm organising a little reading club,' she says. 'I was hoping you boys could pick out five books each that you think would be good for the group. I need some boys to tell me what other boys would like to read.'

'We don't read, miss,' Ryan says. 'Reading's for nerds. Besides, I'm getting out tomorrow and Jamie's got court the day after and he'll probably get out too.'

'Which is all the more reason for your input – so you can help the boys who are still here,' Shae says to Ryan.

'I read books,' I say. 'I've read at least half the Goosebumps books.' I can't help but feel like I'm sticking up for Shae.

'See,' Shae says to Ryan.

'I'll help ya,' I say to Shae.

'Oh, I see what *you're* doing,' Ryan says to me, raising his eyebrows twice. 'Didn't take you for a *horny nerd*, Jamie.'

'Go away.' I head to the bookshelf. All the Percy Jackson books are there, but I'm more excited to find that there are a few Goosebumps books. I take out two – *Scream of the Evil Genie* and *The Beast from the East* – and pop them into the box Shae is carrying.

Ryan scans the bookshelves. He takes a book out and reads the back, then nods and puts it in the box.

I pick up a book called *Into the River* by Ted Dawe. The writing on the back cover makes the book sound interesting, so I put it in the box. I grab another book with a bright red spine and chuck it in.

I come to the poetry section – a collection of slim books on the bottom shelf at the floor. Ryan drops another book into the box and starts complaining to Shae about how boring he's finding this.

A spine catches my eye and I pull it out. *Lemons in the Chicken Wire* by Alison Whittaker. When I open the book, a slip of paper falls out. Printed on the paper is a poem: 'Dreamtime' by Oodgeroo Noonuccal. I skim the first line, then stuff the slip in my pocket.

We pick out some more books and throw them in the box. Ryan delivers his final pick to the box via a basketball throw. Shae thanks us for our help and she and the screw take us through about twenty doors to get some pizza. I have a slice of supreme.

'Get this,' Shae says. 'The pizza shop is called Pizza Shop. How funny's that?'

'Funny? I think we got very different senses of humour, miss,' Ryan teases.

I'm stuffed when I get back to my room. I close the door and drop my shirt to the floor again. I pull the slip from my pocket and lie on my bed. I read over the words: Oodgeroo Noonuccal. I wish I had a name like that – a cool Aboriginal name.

III

Ryan's release day has arrived.

'What's wrong with you?' Ryan asks.

'What? Nothing. Just thinking.' I shake my head and rub my eyes.

'Thinking about what?'

'Nothin',' I say. 'You keen, cuz? Keen to get home?'

'Yep. I'm getting blackout-drunk tonight,' Ryan says, as we sit at the table in the unit, each with a bowl of cornflakes for breakfast. Ryan's fidgeting with his plastic spoon, and his leg is ticking like a clock counting down to the second he can walk out through the gates. I've gotten used to sitting here with Ryan every morning, but today's our last breakfast together.

'That's all you wanna do?' I ask. 'Get drunk?'

'Bruh, I haven't drank for like eight months. I'm desperate.'

'Are you gonna go back to school?'

'Yeah, I spose. I'm more keen to see Teri again.'

'Teri?'

'She works in the house I'm at, comes in every weekend. She's mad fun – we have a good laugh. She's been missing me, I reckon.'

I finish my cornflakes and Ryan finishes his. He licks some milk from his top lip as Shae and two screws come into the unit.

'Time to go, Ryan,' Shae says.

'I'll miss ya, cuz,' I say as we shake hands and share a half-hug.

'Come up for a visit one day,' Ryan says. 'Find me on Facebook and hit me up. We'll have a charge and I'll show ya the city.'

'Yeah, I might. Catch ya.'

Ryan leaves with Shae and the screws. I'm worried about him and happy for him all at once. I hope I don't see him back in here in a few days. As I watch him leave the unit, I suddenly feel all alone again. I got no mates in here now, but court's in a few days. Maybe I'll make bail and I'll walk through the gates like Ryan. Not that I'll last long anyway. The lads will want their revenge.

It makes me nervous, makes my stomach feel sour. I see Mark Cassidy's face, all angry and red, standing over my body as I slowly die.

I try to think of something else, think about Trey saying I used to be a dancer. I try to remember the jingle. 'Hot Potato'. I play it in my head, over and over.

I was eye-level with the TV, singing away as a jingle played. It was 'Hot Potato' by The Wiggles. I was dancing, imitating The Wiggles as they sang.

'Go, Jamie,' Mum said behind me. I did the 'Hot Potato', dancing with my hands balled into fists, tapping them on top of each other. I turned back to see Mum. Her eyes grew smaller because she was smiling so hard, and her hair was long, dark brown and wavy. She was holding her phone up at me, so I turned around and danced for the camera, singing along and hitting every note perfectly — at least in my head, I was hitting the notes perfectly.

The song ended and The Wiggles began 'Fruit Salad'.

'Mum, dance with me,' I said.

'I don't know how to, baby,' she said.

'I'll show you!'

I grabbed her fingers, and my hand was only big enough to wrap around three of them. I tried to yank her up twice before she finally stood. I danced as the song continued and looked to her to make sure she was dancing too. And she was. She was smiling and laughing, her shoulders bobbing to the beat of the song.

'12

September twentieth: court day.

It's fucking hot. I've got no energy at all. I didn't sleep more than a couple of hours last night, and now I'm sweating like a pig in my sticky red polo shirt. The handcuffs don't help either. My wrists are hot in their tight grip, and I swear I'm feeling body heat radiating from the two screws who bring me into a room with a big television with a camera on top at the end of the table. I was meant to call Aunty Dawn before court, but I was straight out of bed and off to the AVL room.

After a while, the black television screen changes to the image of a woman in a grey suit sitting at a table. She's old, like in her forties, probably.

'Hi, Jamie,' she says. 'I'm Trudy. I'll be representing you today.' Trudy has a really squeaky voice. It's the exact opposite of the kind of voice you'd want in a radio presenter.

'Hey.'

'So, we're applying for bail today, as I'm sure you know.'

'Yep.'

'We have one of the tougher magistrates, so I don't want you to get your hopes up.'

'Okay.' I don't pay attention to anything else she says.

'I'll see you soon, Jamie,' Trudy says. 'I want to go over your files again before we go into court.'

My files. I think of the pieces of paper with my name on them, with information about me. I wonder who types up those pages. That person probably thinks they know me, because they've read about my history and the police reports, but they don't know me. Not really.

The screen turns black again, the hours go by and I find myself dozing off against the wall in the video room. I jolt back to life when the television screen comes on again. It's the courtroom. The first thing I notice are the spotless walls. They've been freshly painted white, clear and pure. I swear I can almost smell the paint job.

The screen is split. One half shows the magistrate, seated at the front of the courtroom, where the ground is raised like she is sitting on a stage. She has a wooden bench in front of her, though, so I can only see her chest and head. The magistrate's got on a big black robe which covers her whole body with little pockets for her skinny arms to come out.

In the other half, Trudy is sitting at a long table, and a woman is at the other end. The woman has got a proper suit on, tie and all. She's got short hair and looks almost like a bulldog when she glances up at the camera. Behind Trudy and the bulldog-woman's table, Aunty Dawn is sitting alone in the rows of empty seats. She's wearing a purple dress and a black jacket. Her hair is tied in a ponytail.

'Hi, James,' the magistrate says. 'Can I call you *Jamie*?'

It takes a moment to realise *her honour* is addressing me personally. I give her a nod and a smile.

'Yep.'

'Thanks for joining us,' the magistrate says. I look back to Aunty Dawn. The picture quality on the TV is shit. I wish it was better so I could see her face more clearly.

The magistrate, Trudy and the bulldog-woman mumble legal mumbo jumbo for a while.

They talk and talk and I really don't understand what they are saying. I wouldn't be able to tell anyone if it was going good or bad. All I know is that there's a flow of cool air brushing the back of my neck and it feels wonderful as the bulldog-woman begins her speech.

'Danger to the community,' she says. That I heard. 'Offending behaviour…incidents…damage to the victims…'

I realise I haven't really thought about how Mark Cassidy took the news his car had been stolen. I wonder what went through his head when he saw it banged up, scratches all over the paintwork, damage under the bonnet, cracked windscreen, Lenny's vomit on his back floor. I wonder what went through his head when he learned it was the boys from the Valley – Jamie, Dally and Lenny – who took his birthday gift for a ride and fucked it right up. Maybe he thinks all his racist thoughts and feelings are justified now, that we are all criminals; or if we're not, we are criminals who just haven't done any crimes *yet*. He's probably planning his ultimate revenge, fantasising about bashing our heads in with a block buster because we took away his precious car. I'm sure his daddy would have taken a stroll down to the car yard and got him a new V6 for thirty grand or so. I don't doubt for a second that his daddy would buy him a new car as soon as possible, to heal the hurt he, my *victim*, had been dealt. I know I should probably feel bad about what we did, and I do, just not for him.

'Do you understand, Jamie?' the magistrate asks, and it snaps me out of my thoughts.

'Yep,' I say, nodding.

'Bail is refused...'

Bail is refused.

I wasn't really expecting to get bail, but actually hearing the words feels like a real kick in the balls.

'Thank you,' the magistrate says as she stands. Everyone in the courtroom stands with her. The screen goes black.

The handcuffs come on and I'm going back down the corridors and through the locked doors, along the pavements, through gates and back to the unit.

I head to my room and lie on my bed. The handcuffs are off, but they feel like they're still around my wrists. I may as well be chained to these walls. My chest feels heavy. The thought comes to my mind that I might never leave this place. I want to go home. I want to go back to school. I want to call Aunty Dawn and Uncle Bobby.

There's a knock at the door. Alex is at the window. He opens the door with a smirk on his face. There's another screw behind him. He drops some clothes on the foot of my bed – purple polo, black trackpants.

'You're off to the Purple Unit, mate,' Alex says. 'You'll love it there.'

The Purple Unit.

Ronnie's unit.

I want to ask why, kick the new clothes off my bed and tell him to fuck off.

I want to scream in his face as loud as I can.

I want to break my fists on the wall.

I want to run as fast as I can, but I can't run anywhere.

I get off my bed, change into the purple polo shirt, then follow Alex and the other screw out of my room and out of the unit.

'Catch ya, cuz,' Kevin says from across the courtyard. 'Do the Aboriginal programs and I'll see ya in there.'

'Yeah, might,' I say.

Alex and the other screw bring me out of the Red Unit, through door after door, then across and along the pathways outside the other units.

We walk to the Purple Unit and buzz through the gate.

'Heard you got refused bail,' Alex says quietly, almost whispering. 'You know that was the right decision, yeah? People like you don't change overnight. You're too dangerous to be outside. A long slog will teach you a lesson.'

I shake my head. My fists are clenching and my cheeks are burning. I could burst into flames.

'This is right where you belong,' Alex says, opening the gate to the Purple Unit.

The Purple Unit is bigger than the Red. I notice a few Koori boys kicking a soccer ball in the courtyard. One of the boys is Ronnie. He's wearing trackpants and a black singlet, and I can see how muscly his arms are. He stops when he sees me, stares at me. His eyes are dark and I can feel him watching me as I walk.

I head into the unit, and Alex and the screw show me to my room. There are two beds inside and there's a white boy on the other bed. He gets up when I enter.

'You're sharing with Magnus,' Alex says. 'Don't go bummin' each other in the night.'

Magnus shakes my hand. He's skeleton-skinny. I can see his cheekbones through his skin.

'Enjoy your home in the Purple Unit, Langton,' Alex says.

After Alex and the screw leave, I head to the courtyard. One of the screws is supervising Ronnie and the other boys on the court. I stop at the phone and call Aunty Dawn. It takes four rings, but she answers.

'Hey, Aunt,' I say.

'Oh, Jamie. I'm sorry. I really thought you'd get bail,' Aunty Dawn says.

'It's okay, Aunt. I'm all good. I got moved to another unit.'

'You sure you're okay? Is there someone in there you can talk to? Like a counsellor or something?'

'Yessssss, there's a counsellor, but I don't need that. I'm all good.'

Aunty Dawn sighs. 'Just keep your head up, okay? Don't let that place break you. You'll come out the other end stronger than ever.'

'I know, Aunt.'

'You know it's a bit far to visit, but me and Uncle will try, okay?'

'All good.'

After our phone call, it's lockdown then dinner then bedtime. The beds in the Purple Unit are comfy as well. The pillows are fluffier than they were in the Red Unit. It's a cooler night, with the breeze coming through my little window.

'They don't get it,' Magnus says quietly. 'They don't know you, so they make these guesses on you. Mum didn't say anything about them, though. It's her fault, 'cause she didn't tell you nothin'. Nah.'

He's talking to himself. He must be fucked in the head. I kind of don't want to go to sleep, scared I might wake up to him standing over me.

13

I'm awoken by a bang on my door and my eyes are attacked by the blinding morning light coming through the little window near the ceiling. I sit up and look for Magnus. He's not on his bed.

'Langton, you got a visit,' the screw says as he opens the door to my room.

I spring from bed and wash my face, brush my teeth, then I'm handcuffed and escorted out of the unit. The screw transports me along the pathways and through the locked doors.

Into the visit area, I'm stopped at the glass door and there is Trey sitting on his side of the coffee table. I feel more excited about the day just seeing him there. The screw uncuffs me and opens the door. I walk in and take my seat opposite Trey.

'Jamie, Jamie, Jamie,' he says.

'Trey, Trey, Trey.'

'Sorry about the court outcome.'

I rest my foot on the edge of the coffee table and slouch back in my plastic seat. 'What you sorry for?'

'I don't know,' he says. 'Sorry you have to be stuck in here for longer.'

'It's all right. I was kind of expecting it. I'm all good,' I say.

'You always say that. You're *all good*. How are you really?' he asks. He's got this seriousness about his face now. He's grown more facial hair on his cheeks and his chin.

'I'm fine,' I say, trying to fight back the nervous smile. 'I don't get depressed or anything. Don't worry.'

'Dad gave me a call this morning,' Trey says. 'From the police station.'

Trey is quiet for a moment, waiting for me. He can probably see my hate rising back up. After we were taken from Mum and Dad, the only time we could see them was when they had an appointment and some white person in a suit was there to supervise. They visited for a while, but then it was like they were just gone. They stopped visiting, stopped calling. I guess they knew me and Trey would be all right with Aunty Dawn, that she'd look after us just fine, but it pissed me off somethin' bad.

'What he do this time?' I ask.

'Just drunk in public. He asked to call me when he was being let out. I told him I was coming to visit you today. He wasn't happy when he heard you were in juvie.'

'What's it to him?'

'He wanted me to give you his number, so you can give him a call when you get out,' Trey says. 'If you want, you can catch the bus to Sydney and we can go see him and Mum together.'

'I don't want his number. I got nothing I want to say to him, or her.' I chuckle. Trey sighs, sits back and nods to himself. I feel bad. I think I raised my voice at him. I know he's only passing on a message and I know he's glad to be in touch with Mum and Dad again. I can't help it – the anger comes and I'm right back there at six years old, wondering why Mum and Dad aren't looking after me anymore. I feel the tears force their way to my eyes. I try to hold them in, but they roll out over my eyelids. I don't make a sound, though, just wipe the tears away before they can march down to my cheeks.

'You all right?' Trey asks.

I sniffle. I don't know if I am all right or if I'm terrible or if everything is just a big ball of shit being shoved down my throat every minute I'm awake.

'I'm just not ready,' I say. 'Not yet.'

'That's okay,' Trey says. 'No one is gonna make you. *I'm* not gonna make you. I'm going to see Dad, but whether you do or not is up to you. It's your decision.'

I feel so weak, tearing up in front of Trey. That's what *boys* do, not men. I want Trey to see that I'm a man now too.

The sadness fades away when Trey leaves, and all that is left is anger. I'm angry at my fucking father. What's the point of him even seeing us now? Does he want to apologise? Whatever it is, it doesn't matter. I haven't been his son in years.

The struggling car engine sputtered and coughed and then rolled from the road onto the dirt. I was sitting in the back seat with Trey beside me and Mum and Dad in the front.

'Fuck,' Dad shouted at the steering wheel.

'I told ya to put ten bucks in at Ashcroft,' Mum said. She looked back at us. Her brown eyes were tired and her hair was long and messy, unbrushed. 'It's okay, my babies,' she said to me and Trey, and I could smell grog on her breath. Grog-breath filled the car.

'Shut it,' Dad said to Mum. He twisted the keys in the ignition and they jingled like wind as he turned them. The car coughed and buffered forward before wheezing out of power.

'Why don't you ever listen to me?' Mum asked Dad. 'Now we're stuck all the fuckin' way out 'ere.'

'Shut the fuck up,' Dad shouted, and he bashed his fists on the steering wheel.

Trey gasped.

The car rocked and Dad kept shouting, hammering the steering wheel. I looked out the window to the dark grey clouds above the bush, above our car off the side of the road somewhere in the middle of nowhere. I just wanted to go home. I wanted to be in my bed. I felt scared – something bad was gonna happen.

14

I'm back in the unit.

I can still hear the jiggling keys and my father shouting.

I can smell the grog-breath.

Feel the dread in my stomach

Because Mum and Dad are arguing instead of trying to get us home.

I go to my room.

Close the door.

I plant my face into my pillow and scream.

I scream as hard as I can.

Then the tears come

And I punch my mattress over and over and over.

At afternoon rec time

I wish Ryan was still here.

I wish I was still in the Red Unit with him.

I head outside, sit on one of the picnic tables.

A screw's sitting across from me.

She's watching the boys playing with the basketball.

In my head, I'm begging her not to talk to me.

I catch her in the corner of my eye.

I know it's only a matter of time.

'How are you going, mate?' she asks.

I sigh as loud as I've ever sighed.

I stand.

I walk towards the boys:

My roomie, Magnus, a few white boys, a few Kooris

And Ronnie.

One of the screws is shooting hoops with them.

One of the boys shoots, but the ball ricochets off the backboard.

The ball bounces.

Magnus gets it.

Ronnie shoulders him and takes the ball for himself.

Ronnie looks like the Hulk standing next to Magnus.

'Hey,' Magnus calls, but Ronnie turns his back to him.

Ronnie shoots and lands the shot.

Another boy gets the ball, dribbles back to the crack in the ground they are using as the free-throw line.

Magnus shakes his head and walks towards the unit.

I start towards Ronnie and the other boy.

'Chuck us the ball,' I say.

Ball lands in my hands.

I shoot from fifteen metres out.

The ball hits the ring and bounces away.

'Shit shot,' Ronnie says.

The first thing he's ever said to me.

Shit shot.

Ronnie dribbles the ball

Back to where I am.

He shoots.

Ball hits the backboard

And misses.

'Shit shot yourself,' I say.

'What you say, boy?' Ronnie asks, turning to me.

He's taller than me.

Towers over me.

Steps towards me.

I should step back, step away.

No.

I stand my ground.

'You said I was a shit shot, but you missed it too.'

'Get fucked,' he says.

Ronnie shoves me.

I'm falling.

My foot stops me.

'*You* get fucked,' I say.

I start for the unit.

Ronnie's laughing.

HaHaHaHaHa.

Spit hits the back of my neck.

Ronnie's spit.

'Leave him, Ronnie,' a screw says behind us.

'We're just playin', bruh,' Ronnie says. 'Come back, bruh, we were just gettin' started.'

I head into the unit.

Boys at the table playing cards.

Eyes turn to me.

I wish Ryan was here.

He'd jump up.

He'd have my back.

'Let's have a go, then,' Ronnie says. 'Reckon you could knock me? Come on, let's have a go.'

Hallway.

To my room.

Open the door.

Magnus is sitting on his bed.

A shove on my back

Hits like a wrecking ball.

Freefall towards my bed.

My ankle whacks the post.

Magnus springs to his feet.

'Ronnie!' I hear one of the screws yell.

'Get up, lad,' Ronnie says.

I stand tall.

Step towards him.

He's a giant.

'Fuck off,' I say.

'Don't be a pussy,' he says.

Fire in my chest.

Hot.

Heat.

Fists clench tight.

My fingernails stab my palms.

Arms on Ronnie

And shove him into the wall.

He's so strong.

Swings me to the floor.

The floor in the doorway.

Ronnie on top of me.

Bang on my face.

Raise my arms.

Shield.

His fists like rocks.

Bang on my arms.

Ronnie falls over me.

Carpet burns my elbows as I shuffle.

Me on top.

Elbow like a hammer.

Over and over.

Voices everywhere.

Shouting.

Cheering.

Cooing.

Into the hallway.

To the office.

Limping.

Ankle throbbing.

Footsteps booming.

Bang on my back.

Carpet burns my cheek

As I land and slide with

Ronnie on top of me.

Swearing.

Yelling.

Yanking.

White hands on my shoulders.

Roll to my side.

White hands lift me to my feet.

Screws.

Men.

Over screws' shoulders

White hands punch Ronnie.

White hands shove Ronnie against

The wall.

His chin grates the white wall as

White hands grasp his head, envelop his skull.

White tight grip on my arms.

'Get the fuck off me,' I shout.

All in.

All the boys.

Fists flying.

Shouting.

Yelling.

Like a tug of war.

White fists on black jaws.

On children's jaws.

Dizzy.

Ears are hot.

Screws rush away.

Card and keys in my hands.

In the office, a screw speaking into her lapel.

All screws locked in the office.

Boys shoulder the door

But it won't open.

Everyone is puffing.

Chests are heaving.

They all have that look in their eyes:

The one I saw in Dally's eyes

The night we took Mark Cassidy's Mitsubishi.

It is the look of thrill.

We are doing something we have never done before

And nothing can stop us.

More screws through the window.

Two on their radios.

Magnus beside me.

His eye is bruised.

A little cut at the top of his cheekbone.

My purple shirt is ripped around the collar.

'Look out,' Magnus says.

Through the big doors of the unit's entrance

The screws are gathering behind the gates.

Pads and helmets.

Batons.

Riot gear.

I don't know what to do.

I wish Dally was here.

He would know what to do.

He would lead us.

'I'm not going down without a fight,' Ronnie says. 'They comin' at us with everything, by the looks of it. We'll take 'em on.'

All eyes on Ronnie.

One of the big boys in the back turns away and walks to his room,

But no one else moves.

'We don't have to fight them,' I say.

I hold up my hand and

Show them the set of keys with a swipe card attached.

Ronnie's eyes light up.

The screws grow in number on the other side of the glass doors.

I take the keys and

Rush up the hallway of the unit.

'Come on,' I shout back to all the boys.

Ankle is aching.

Burning.

Cracking.

Swipe card on black pad.

Bzzzzzzz.

Door clicks open.

Run.

Footsteps pounding on the hard floor.

Across the courtyard.

Drainage pipe leads to the roof.

Screws flooding the unit.

Grip the pipe.

Lift myself up.

Climb to the top.

Steel roof is warm.

Reach back down.

Lift Magnus up.

Then Ronnie.

Then another Koori kid

And another.

Five of us on the roof.

Army of screws rush into the outside courtyard.

They tackle the boys waiting to climb.

So many screws.

Clustering on top of them all.

The boys

Fight back

But

The screws are too strong.

Men's hands on boys' heads.

Push them into the ground.

Hands twisted behind boys' backs.

Strap on handcuffs.

I can't stand the sight:

Big men

Beating the hell out of

Small boys.

I gaze over the roof.

Looking for anything.

Metal spinning roof turbine.

I kick at it with my good ankle and my crappy shoes.

I kick it out of place and pick it up.

Back to the edge of the roof.

Aim for the screw on one of the boys' backs.

Launch the turbine.

It pings the back of his helmet.

He turns up to me.
All the screws drag the boys away inside.
I sit down on the roof.
I catch a breath.
I lie back.
There's not a cloud in the sky.

15

The sun is starting to set over the hills in the distance while I'm on the roof with the boys. I'm walking, following the gutters all the way around the edges. I can see the whole juvie centre from the roof, all the units and walkways and buildings. I can see the pool near the big hall. Over the tall steel fences with barbed wire on their tops, you can see cars rolling along the highway. I can see the sign for the Maccas not too far away. I could go for some Maccas right now. I didn't have breakfast because I woke up late, then I didn't eat lunch because I was too pissed off, and now we are nearing dinnertime and I'm starving.

I turn to the boys who made it onto the roof. There's a white boy with blond hair and a tall, skinny, Koori boy; both boys I don't know yet. I stop beside the Koori boy.

'What's your name?' I ask him.

'Eric,' he says.

'Where you from?'

'North Sydney,' he says. 'Cremorne.'

I take a seat on the warm roof. I kick off my shoes and massage my sore ankle.

Magnus sits beside me and lies back. Ronnie is pacing around the roof, mumbling some Kendrick Lamar lyrics to himself.

'This was dumb,' Magnus says.

'You know what, brother?' I say. 'I'm starting to think the same thing.'

'How long you in for?' Eric asks me.

'Dunno. Haven't been sentenced yet.'

'True? This is my eighth time. I came in first when I was eleven.'

Eric has the blackest Koori accent I've ever heard. Even though he's from North Sydney, he speaks like he grew up in the bush.

'Eleven? That's fucked,' I say.

'Yeah, my cousin got locked up when he was ten,' Eric says. 'And his sister was eleven when she first went in.'

I piss myself, imagining a little ten-year-old kid being marched off in handcuffs, being forced into a coloured polo shirt and crappy cheap shoes, locked up in juvie. It blows my mind. Doesn't feel right. I try to imagine myself at ten years old, being marched through the corridors and locked doors. I'd probably piss my pants right there on the carpet before the admissions desk.

'You play footy?' I ask.

'Yeah, played back home when I was younger,' Eric says.

'You should see this lad Kevin in the Red Unit,' I say. 'He's the fastest blackfulla I know. He could sidestep a train.'

Eric chuckles to himself.

'I went all right. Played rep a few times, but I just wanted to drink and do stupid shit more than I wanted to play footy,' Eric says. 'I never woulda made it.'

'You don't know that,' I say. 'What position you play?'

'Centre.'

'Yeah, you're a big fulla, like Greg Inglis. You should quit the shit when you get out,' I say. 'You already live in Sydney, so you got a good chance anyway.'

Eric shakes his head. 'Don't think I could quit the shit,' he says. 'Don't think I want to.'

'Boys,' someone says from below. I crawl over to the edge of the roof and peer down. Two of the screws are standing there on the ground with their riot gear all over their bodies. 'Why don't you all come down now? It's been a couple of hours.'

'Get us some food, ay? Then we'll think about it,' Ronnie says.

'If we get you some food, you'll come down?' the screw asks. I can hardly make out his face behind the plastic shield stretching down from his helmet.

'We said *get us food* and *we'll think about it*,' I say, realising I'm backing up Ronnie now, who just sort of walks away and continues humming to himself.

Soon enough, the screws bring some packets of potato chips and throw them up to us. They throw us three bottles of water, too. I share mine with Eric.

The sun sets. The darkness is coming and it is starting to get cold on the roof. I sit with my knees to my chest to

147

stop myself from shivering. Eric paces back and forth and breathes into his hands.

'No surprise. The monkeys love to climb,' a voice calls from below. 'It's nice and warm inside. Getting cold out here.'

Magnus follows me to the edge of the roof. It's Alex standing there below us with his riot gear on – padded vest, baton in one hand.

'Come on down, Langton. I'll take it easy on you,' Alex says.

'Go fuck yourself,' I say back.

Another screw comes out of the building and barges through the army of kitted-up screws to Alex. He grabs Alex by the shoulder and they look like they're having the quietest argument in the world. Alex shakes his head and goes back inside the unit.

'I'm gonna head down,' Magnus says. I nod at him. 'I'm coming,' he calls to the screws. He starts climbing down and the white boy with blond hair follows him. The screws wait for them at the bottom. I watch from the edge as they land in the arms of the screws. The screws push them against the wall, on their stomachs, but they aren't too rough. They cuff their hands behind their backs and take them inside.

I sit back up and look over to Ronnie and Eric. They seem just as tired as I am. I feel like all the anger I had has been used up. I'm empty. I open the last packet of plain potato chips. I shove a few into my mouth. I pass them to Eric.

'I might head down,' Eric says, crunching the chips in his mouth. 'I can't sleep up here, and I need to take a shit.'

'No worries,' I say.

I shake his hand and then stand at the edge of the roof. I watch Eric climb down the pipe. Four screws pounce on him as soon as his feet hit the ground. They shove him into the wall and cuff his hands behind his back. They take him inside and two screws stay behind, looking up to me.

Now it's just me and Ronnie. We both sit against the sides of an airconditioner.

'Ryan told me you been in and out of here for years,' I say. 'You like it in 'ere?'

Ronnie takes a breath. 'What's it to you?'

'Just makin' conversation.'

We're quiet for another minute. I look to the clouds. They're all orange and purple. It's really pretty, actually, like a poem in an abstract kind of way. I almost open my mouth to tell Ronnie.

'On the outs, I got nothin'.' Ronnie sighs. 'I can't get a job, got no money. In 'ere, I can kick back with my mates, I get free food and a bed guaranteed. It's not as bad in here as it is on the outs. The world's shit out there.'

'You reckon?'

'Yeah. If you don't think so, maybe you got stuff goin' for you.'

Ronnie stands and heads to the pipe. I smile and Ronnie frowns at me.

'What's so funny?' Ronnie asks.

'I just remembered,' I say. 'I was on a camp a couple of months ago, and the youth worker asked what our goals were before the end of the year. I told him my goal was to not die.'

I giggle again and Ronnie shakes his head. 'You won't die.' He climbs down the pipe and now I'm on the roof by myself.

After all the punches I threw today, and the punches I took, the rush in my blood when I raced up the hallway with the keys and got us outside, the strength I used to pull the boys up onto the roof with me, I am exhausted.

I look over the clouds of the darkening sky. It's all Dad's fault. He's still ruining my life, making me go mental, making me do all this stupid shit. I'm fucked because of him, and he just left and didn't come back. I would never do that to my kids. I know I wouldn't. I'd be a good dad. I'd always be there.

A tear breaks away from my eye as I stare at the edge of the roof. I don't wipe it away like I did when I started tearing up in front of Trey. I just let the tears burn my eyes and march down my cheeks. I lick my lips and taste the salt.

I watch the gutters of the roof, expecting a couple of screws to climb up and see me crying here, but rough me up anyway, cuff me and shove me against walls, force their knees into my back. Maybe I could just jump off. It's not super high, but if I land the right way, I might break my neck. Maybe then I'll stop being a waste of space. I reckon I could do it.

I stand, walk to the gutter and gaze down. Three screws look up to me. Not today. Even if I did jump, they would probably catch me. Then they would put me on suicide watch, or something like that. But maybe Ronnie was right – maybe I've got *something* going for me on the outside because I don't think of this place as a good place. No way. This is a dark place. This is the shittest place to be.

'I'm coming down,' I say.

'Good boy,' one of the screws says.

Good boy.

I guess they'll beat the shit out of me because of what I've done. Maybe they'll kill me. I hate Ronnie, but I hope he's right. I hope I don't fail my camp-goal.

I lower my legs and take a hold of the pipe, shuffle over, then a strong grip around my ankle brings me down.

16

The rooms are smaller in Segregation.

White paint over bricks.

It's morning.

The blanket is warm over my body.

'Breakfast,' the screw says.

He's tall and kitted up.

My room door opens.

Screw hands me buttered toast on a paper plate.

'How about some bacon and eggs?' I ask.

He scoffs, locks the door when he leaves.

I think I have been in here two days now, two wake-ups.

The toast is moist and soft.

Not even toasted to an acceptable amount of toasty-ness.

The butter is thick.

They lobbed it all on without even smoothing it out.

It wouldn't have killed them to dab on some Vegemite.

I stay in my room because that's all I can do.

The white walls are decorated in graffiti scratched into
the paint.

The tags of boys I won't ever know.

Their nicknames, I guess.

Jezzy. ANto. Clixy.

My bed isn't even comfy.

The mattress is thin.

I can feel the springs of the bed right through it.

III

The next morning arrives.

I slept a few hours.

Probably a few hours.

I dunno.

I'm still tired when breakfast is served.

This time, it's some healthy cereal

With sultanas and shit.

I don't like it too much.

Eleven o'clock.

Screw comes to my door.

Door unlocks.

He's got on his vest and kneepads and face shield.

'Rec time,' he says.

Hands cuffed at my front.

Walk out of my room.

Concrete courtyard.

Concrete floors,

Concrete walls.

Metal picnic table bolted to the concrete.

There are no colours here.

My polo shirt is black now.

There is a dusty smell in the air.

None of the other boys are allowed out when I am.

The cuffs aren't too tight.

There are a couple of other boys in Segro, locked in their rooms.

Ronnie's lying on his bed as I pass.

Another boy is pacing by his door.

Tall Eric is doing push-ups against his wall.

'Eric, brother,' I call out. I walk over to his room and stand by the door. 'What's happenin'?'

'Nothin' at all,' he says, puffing.

'How long we in here for?' I ask.

He shrugs his shoulders.

'Could be a week, could be a month. Last time, I was in Segro for four months.'

'Four months? Fuck.'

'Step away from his door, Langton,' the screw says.

I don't go right away, but I head back to the table with slow steps.

There is a basketball hoop at the end of the courtyard.

I could've thrown some hoops if I wasn't handcuffed.

Segro is such a shitty place.

Rec time ends.

I'm uncuffed and locked back in my room.

The screw walks away and I bang my head against the wall.

Not because I want to hurt myself or anything, but because I want to stop thinking.

I bang my head again and think maybe I'll knock myself out.

Maybe I'll hit my head too hard,

Bruise my brain or break my skull,

Then these memories –

Of Trey, Mum and Dad –

Will stop coming back.

Ham and lettuce sandwiches for dinner.

Darkness afterwards, except for a little light in the courtyard.

Ruckus happening in the other units.

Distant voices yell out to each other.

Not very loud.

On my bed, I stare at the ceiling.

Footsteps click on the ground.

Click.

Click.

Click.

They stop at my door.

Alex's face in the little window.

I sit up.

'You still got a job?' I say.

'Of course I do,' Alex says. 'I don't have a criminal record.'

Alex smirks.

His face is in shadow, but I still see it.

'Segro suits you,' Alex says. 'This is the best place for someone like you.'

Then he's gone.

Bad places attract bad men.

He's a bad man.

Evil man.

I could kill him.

III

Another day passes.

Then another day.

Another day of sitting and lying.

Another day of bland sandwiches.

Another day of white walls.

A week passes quickly.

Maybe a week?

Who knows?

Who cares?

A new morning.

I'm awoken by a knock at my door.

The screws are there, peering in at me through the window.

'Langton, you got a visit.'

I know it's Trey.

'I don't want it,' I say.

III

The day drags on and I'm just lying on my bed.

I try lying with my arm behind my head, but it's too uncomfortable to hold for too long, so I turn on my side.

After a ham sandwich for lunch, the screws let me out for rec time.

I'm sitting at the table in my handcuffs when Shae comes in through a door on the other side of the courtyard. She walks over with her big, purely happy smile, and takes a seat opposite me at the metal table.

'Hey, Jamie, you up for a quick chat?' she asks.

'Sure. I'm not too busy.'

Shae rests her hands on the table and interlaces her fingers like she's about to say a prayer.

'I hear you declined your brother's visit. Is everything all right?' she asks.

'Yesssss,' I say. 'All good.'

'Did something happen? Is there a reason you don't want to see him?'

The handcuffs clang on the table as I bring my hands to my forehead.

'Nah, nothin' happened. I'll see him soon.'

'Is it because of the incident on the roof?'

'Nooooo, it's not because of the roof thing,' I say, rubbing my eyes with my thumbs. I scratch the sides of my nose and look to the other locked rooms.

'Some of the boys in here don't get many visits, if any,' Shae says. 'It's good for you, *now* especially, to have your big brother visiting you.'

'I know,' I say, bringing my hands back to the table with a clang. 'It's just...he wants me to see my dad, and I don't want to see him. Besides, I'm locked up. I'm a crim. I'm shit. It's not like he can help me or anything. He doesn't care about me. Not really. I'm no use to him.'

Shae plants an elbow on the table and rests her cheek in her hand, looking over me with those brown eyes. Alex's smirk comes to my mind, his face blanketed in shadow when he stood at my door last night. I want to tell Shae about him, how he's tormenting me.

'Do you want to talk about your parents? About your dad?' Shae asks. 'What about your mum? What's her name?'

'Kate,' I say.

'What's your happiest memory of your mum?' Shae asks.

I bring my thumbs to my eyes again. 'I don't know.'

'You sure?'

'Can't think of anything right now.'

Shae hums to herself for a moment.

'My happiest memory of *my* mum was when I was ten,' she says. 'We went to the Easter Show together. All we did was eat chocolates and go on rides and laugh and smile. God, we laughed so much that weekend.'

I look to Shae, look into her eyes. They are glassy, like they're about to start watering as she talks about going to the Easter Show with her mum.

'Well, I've gotta go, but I'll come back and see you soon. Maybe see your brother when he comes in for another visit. Might be good for you, yeah? Segro isn't known for keeping the spirits up.'

'Yeah. Maybe.'

Shae leaves and I'm just sitting there at the table, still trying to think of my happiest memory of Mum, annoyed that Shae brought her up and took my mind off telling her about Alex.

I'm still trying to think of a memory when rec time is over and I'm back in my room.

After dinner, I lie on my bed and stare at the ceiling again. I wonder what day of the week it is. It feels like a Thursday, but I don't know. I guess it doesn't matter.

It's like I'm standing on a beach with my feet buried in the sand. This big wave comes over me and hits me and takes me under and I can't not cry anymore. The tears flow. I don't even know why I'm crying at this point. It's all just fucked in my head. How many days have I been staring at walls in Segro? How many weeks? I want to go home. I want to go back to Dalton's Bay. I want to see Dally and Lenny again. I want to feel the hardwood floor beneath my feet at Aunty Dawn's house. I want to see Uncle Bobby.

It's all fucked. I'm fucked.

Midnight comes and I'm still not ready to sleep yet. I get up and go to my clothes basket. I go through my pairs of shorts, checking the pockets on two of them before I find the slip of paper with Oodgeroo Noonuccal's poem on it. It's been through the wash, but the ink is still there. I read it again, trying to use the little bit of light that gets in from the outside light-post, but it's too difficult to light the page. I rest back on my pillow and read it in the dark. I finish it, then I read it again.

Then it comes to me – my happiest memory of Mum.

I see her face.

A loud bang followed by crackling.

Mum gasps in shock, then she smiles and laughs.

It was the first night of the Dalton's Bay Carnival, which takes place over a weekend every year in February.

'But Dally's going,' I said to Mum.

'I told ya, we got no money for it,' Mum said. 'What do you want me to do? Run next door and ask 'em for a loan?'

I went back to my room and cried. Trey came in and sat on the side of my bed.

'What's your problem?' he asked.

'Why don't we ever have money?'

'It's not Mum and Dad's fault,' Trey said. 'It's fourteen bucks for a kid just to walk through the gate.'

I didn't care. I cried myself to sleep, hating Mum and Dad for not taking us to the carnival.

The next day I had accepted the fact that we couldn't go, but I just sat in my room all day. We had chicken nuggets for dinner and then Mum left the room and came back holding a folded blanket.

'Come on,' Mum said. 'We'll go watch the fireworks.'

I sighed. 'I thought we got no money.'

She grabbed my shoes, placed them at my feet. A smile came over my face and I pulled on my shoes. Dad wasn't home to come with us, but I didn't care.

The sun was setting by the time we got to the showgrounds. Through the gates, I could see the rides. People were screaming as they rode the Hurricane, and there were heaps of people lined up for the dodgem cars. Kids and adults were walking around with fairy floss and cups of hot chips.

Just outside the gates, Mum rested our blanket on a hill.

'We aren't going in?' I asked Mum.

'No, baby. Maybe next year.'

Trey sat on the blanket with Mum. I sat on the other side of her and it was cold, so Mum wrapped her arms around me and Trey and held us tight. We huddled together as we looked through the fence. We watched the kids and teenagers on the rides, gazed over the flashing lights, heard the screams of joy.

I was a little sad that we weren't inside the gates, but when the fireworks began, I looked to the sky and felt nothing but joy. To Mum, I shouted, 'Wow!'

An especially loud bang in the sky shocked her and she gasped, then she smiled and laughed. I looked back up. All the colours you could imagine were exploding in the sky. I didn't care that we couldn't go in anymore. I didn't care about anything except my mum's arm around my body as we watched the fireworks together. I was happy.

17

The screws escort me through all the doors and corridors and walkways and into the visitors' area. We stop at one of the non-contact rooms and Trey is sitting on the other side of the glass.

The screws unlock the door and take off my handcuffs. I step into the box and they lock the door behind me.

'Jamie, Jamie, Jamie,' Trey says.

'Trey, Trey, Trey.'

'I was starting to worry about ya.'

'Were you missing me?' I ask.

'I wouldn't say *missing*. So, why were you declining all my visits there for a little while?'

'I dunno,' I say. 'I was still in bed a couple times. I just didn't feel like it the other times. It wasn't that long of a while.'

'It was over a month,' Trey says.

'No way,' I say.

'Yeah, it's December now. I didn't see you all of November.'

'Far out. It's December? What's the date?'

'Eighth of December,' Trey says.

I rub the invisible beard on my chin. 'I didn't even realise. I've been in here for four months? That's fucked. It's hard to keep track of the dates when you're lookin' at these walls.'

'What's been happening?' Trey asks.

'Well,' I say, taking a deep breath. 'There was an *incident*, and now I'm in Segregation. I'm that bored all day.'

'Yeah, I heard about what happened,' Trey says.

'It was pretty stupid.'

'Was it your idea?'

'Kind of,' I say. 'I guess. I dunno. You should know by now that I don't really have any plans, I just do shit.'

'I was feeling bad, because it happened after my last visit.'

I realise Trey must have thought he set me off. And he did, in a way, but it's not his fault – it's our parents' fault.

'You don't want to be Humpty Dumpty again, do you?'

'What?'

'Remember? You were climbing on the railing and fell down the stairs out the front of home. Dad rushed you to the hospital and they glued you back together and we called you Humpty Dumpty for a while.'

'Fuck.' I giggle. 'I forgot all about that.'

'All I'm saying is, don't do stupid shit like climb on the roof. You could've really hurt yourself.'

Trey's sounding serious now. Frustrated, even.

'Calm down. I won't be doing that again,' I say.

Trey shakes his head. 'Don't tell me to calm down.'

'It won't happen again,' I say. 'So, what's new with you?'

Trey sits forward and sighs.

'Nothing, really. Me and Jacob are trying to get a new house. We've got this other housemate at the moment. He's a friend of ours, but it feels like it's time to get our own place, you know?'

'Yeah, fair enough. Where you looking?' I ask.

'Probably in the Inner West this time, like Newtown, Erskineville areas.'

'Why you wanna move there?' I ask.

'It's good there,' he says. 'The people, the crowds, it's more our style.'

I shift the stool over to the side and lean against the wall.

'Yeah, fair enough.'

'You can come visit us,' Trey says. 'We're looking for a three-bedroom place.'

'Why do you need three bedrooms?'

'Just in case we have visitors, or, you know, in case you might wanna move in with me.'

'Really?'

Trey sits forward.

'Yeah. You can come live with your big brother. I'll take over the *care* or whatever they call it. I've already talked to your caseworker about it. If you're keen, they'd just need to do an assessment on me and Jacob, then you're good to go.'

I think about what it would be like to live with Trey again. I think we've both changed a fair bit since we last lived together, so it might be weird.

'I've got all my mates in DB,' I say.

'Yeah, I know.' Trey clears his throat. 'I visited Mum and Dad.'

'You did?'

'Yeah. Me and Jacob drove up to their place in The Entrance. They're in a little one-bedroom unit. It was good to be there. They look pretty different now. Different from what you'd probably remember. Have you thought any more about seeing them?'

'Not really,' I say. 'I dunno.'

I sit back and look to the ceiling, study the white lines where the paint wasn't smoothed over well enough, to get my mind off Trey visiting my parents. I think about the toast the screws served me a little while ago, with the butter just lobbed on top.

III

Another week has passed in Segro when a screw comes to my door just after breakfast.

'You're moving to the Blue Unit,' she says. I notice the folded blue polo shirt in her hands. It's the same girl who brought me to the Red Unit.

'Today?'

'Yep. Come along, I'll take you there now.'

I smile as I toss away my black polo shirt and pull on a blue one, then I stuff the slip of paper with the Oodgeroo Noonuccal poem into my pocket.

The screw handcuffs me and we walk with another screw through all the locked doors and corridors to the walkway between units. We pass by the Purple Unit, then the Red, then the Orange Unit.

'There are less boys in the Blue Unit,' the screw says as we walk. 'The decision-makers had to split up the fellas who were on the roof with ya, and they thought it would be best to settle you into the Blue Unit.'

As we pass by the Green Unit, I peer through the steel fences and see a familiar face. A black face. A face I know.

'Is that you, Lenny?' I shout.

He's sitting by the fence in a green polo and he turns to see me. It's Lenny, all right. He's ended up in here. I want nothing more in this moment than to talk to him, to ask him how he is doing, to see if he is all right. He looks healthy, fine. He's alive. He's there and I can see him with my own eyes.

But while I'm smiling at the sight of him, Lenny doesn't smile back. He gives me a blank stare, then frowns.

'Lenny?' I call again. He doesn't react, doesn't call back. He turns his face away from me and I want to call out to him again, but the screws push me along.

The next block is coloured blue on the outside. The unit itself looks smaller, and the courtyard is smaller too. I follow the screws inside and the boys are playing cards around a table with one of the other screws. There are seven boys and only one of them is Koori. The rest are white boys. They all turn to look at me as I enter, and I see one of the white boys whisper something to another.

We arrive at my room and it's smaller, just like the building and the courtyard. I lie on my bed and the screw says something before they leave, but I can't pay attention because I'm remembering Lenny's face. I can't stop thinking about it. He wasn't excited to see me. He hates me. He blames me and he's right to. He wishes he never met me. He wishes we were never friends. He wouldn't be in this mess if we weren't mates. It's my fault he's behind that fence wearing that green polo shirt. It's all my fault.

18

It's my sixth morning in the Blue Unit. I head to the phone instead of to the breakfast table. The automatic message plays through the phone and then Aunty Dawn's voice spills into my ear.

'Go flip the eggs. Quick, I'm on the phone,' she says.

'Aunt?'

'Sorry, Jamie. Just telling Uncle what to do like usual.'

'Lenny's in here,' I say, leaning against the wall of the unit.

'Your *mate* Lenny?'

'Yeah, he's in the Green Unit. We aren't allowed to mix, but I saw him there when they were moving me to the Blue Unit. I called out to him, but he didn't call back to me. Honestly, he looked angry to see me, like he hates me or something. You reckon he's pissed at me?'

'I don't know, son.'

'Have you heard anything about Dally?' I ask.

'No, I haven't. Don't worry about them, just focus on yourself right now. You really need to start thinking about your future,' Aunty Dawn says. 'You know it's not gonna look good for you when you're older if you keep getting locked up. Where do you want to be in ten years' time, son?'

'I want to be on a beach somewhere, with two million in my bank account,' I say. Aunty Dawn sighs. 'I don't know where I'll be in ten years. I don't think that far ahead.'

'You know where I used to work before I retired?' Aunty Dawn asks.

'Yeah,' I say. 'Family Services.'

'I've seen this same story play out a thousand times before,' she says. 'There's only so much I can do, and the rest has to come from you.'

'Okay, Aunt.'

'Do you understand what I'm saying?' she asks.

I don't know if I do, but I say, 'Yeah.'

'I know it's hard to accept it right now, but your mother and father love you. You can avoid them for as long as you want and I'll never force you to see them – unless you're ready – but your parents will always be a part of who you are.'

'Okay, Aunt,' I say. I hang up – the phone clinks as I bang it back into place.

I head back into the common room and sit down with a bowl of cornflakes. Outside, the gate of the unit creaks as it opens. Through the glass doors, two screws walk across the courtyard with a new kid. He's short and skinny and Koori. As the screws bring him into the common room, I realise it's Ryan. His eyes are dark and his hair is longer and frizzly.

'Ryan,' I say, standing from my seat as the screws bring him past us. He turns to me and stares blankly for a moment, almost like he doesn't recognise me. Then his eyes light up.

'Jamie, brother,' he says. The screws take him down the hall and show him to his room.

Ryan sleeps for most of the day. I can hear his snores from the common room and later from the courtyard when I shoot some hoops with one of the screws.

At lunchtime, I notice Shae in the courtyard, talking with a screw kitted up in his riot gear. I head out to her and the screw stands between us.

'As if I'd attack Shae,' I say.

'It's okay,' Shae says to the screw. 'Jamie. Just the man I wanted to see. We're going to do that reading program now if you'd like to come along? You did help pick out the books, after all.'

'I saw my mate Lenny,' I say. 'He's in the Green Unit. I was wondering if I could talk to him.'

'Well,' Shae says, 'Lenny is one of your co-accused. Unfortunately, that means we can't have you guys in the same room together.'

'Why? We're not dangerous or anything.'

'I know,' she says. 'It's just the rules. I'm sorry.'

I wish I could just

Bust through the unit gates

Race across the pathways

Climb the fence

Run into the Green Unit

Find his room and
Lock myself inside with him.
Then I'd tell him how sorry I am
How I hope he doesn't hate me.
I'd tell him I miss him,
That he's a great mate.

'I spoke to your brother, Trey, after your last visit,' she says. 'He told me about your father's cancer.'

I sigh. 'Great.'

Shae is quiet for a moment. 'I'm sorry,' she says.

'Sorry for what?'

'I didn't realise that's why your dad and mum want to see you again. You still don't want to visit them?'

'Nah. No point,' I say. 'They don't even know me.'

'Jamie, I know it's none of my business, but remember I told you that story about my mum, when we went to the Easter Show? My mum died a year later when I was eleven,' Shae says. 'She had a heart attack at forty. There was no warning or anything, she just died one day.'

'Oh, shit. I'm sorry.'

'It's okay,' Shae says. 'I just wanted to say that you only get one mum and one dad, you know? It's probably hard to see that right now, but they do love you and you love them. You might think differently soon. I hope you do.'

'Maybe,' I say.

'So, do you want to come along to the reading program?' she asks.

'Nah, I'm good.'

I am just fucking angry now.

Trey ratted me out, telling Shae our business behind my back.

Shae is trying to guilt me into changing my mind.

She's wrong.

I don't love them.

I stopped loving them a long time ago.

I wish I could yell that at her, then she would shut up about it.

I walk across the courtyard.

Back into my room.

Screw locks me in.

I'm pacing around the room.

My heart is racing.

19

Dinnertime comes.

I head out to the common area.

Alex is leaning against the counter.

He smirks as I take a plate.

Can't deal with his shit right now.

I head to the table. Ryan's there, stuffing vegetables soaked in gravy into his mouth. He smiles when he sees me, but his eyes are droopy and tired.

'So, what you doin' back in 'ere?' I ask, sitting down next to him.

'Are you really that surprised, Langton?' Alex asks, still smirking with that annoying fucking face of his.

'Err, they got me on a robbery in company,' Ryan says, his voice quiet and low. He's not the cheery boy he was when I first came into this place. 'I was off my head at the time. Just stupid, bruh.'

He looks like a neglected puppy. His blue polo shirt shows how skinny he's become – it is at least three sizes too big. If he took off his shirt, I'm sure he'd look like a skeleton with a brown coat draped over its bones.

'You right, cuz?'

'Yeah, all good,' he says.

As we finish eating, Alex approaches the table with his fucking smirk, towering over us.

'Time for bed.'

I knew he was fit, but as he stands over me and Ryan, we can see his muscles bulging through his shirt.

'We're talking,' I say.

'Talking time's over. Time for bed.'

'We're not little fucking kids, you know? You don't have to talk to us like we're children.'

'Why don't you people ever listen?' Alex asks. 'It's bedtime. Be good boys and get to your rooms.'

Ryan stands from the table.

My skin is hot.

Growing hotter by the second.

Fire raging inside me.

Thinking of Trey, Shae,

Trying to get me to see Dad.

Thinking of Lenny

Who hates me.

'I'm over your shit, bruh. Stop talking to us like we're fucking babies,' I say.

Can't control it.

Fire in my arm.

His teeth grind when my fist connects.

In the blink of an eye

My cheek whacks concrete ground.

Knee sharp on my back,

Burning my spine,

Stabbing me with his weight.

'Get off,' I shout.

All the breath in my body leaves through my mouth.

A bang on the back of my head.

'I was right about you,' Alex says, puffing. 'This is where you belong.'

I'm seeing blurry.

Legs of screws and their boots booming on the ground.

Ryan's voice.

Ryan yelling.

Blackness.

Laughter.

Laughter from my mouth.

I'm laughing.

Wrists stinging.

Tight handcuffs around them.

Arm twisting, could be breaking.

Dusty gravel and dirt sticking to my cheek.

Focus.

Forget the pain, and focus.

Focus on breathing.

Breathing.

Breathe in, breathe out.

Breathe in, breathe out.

Can't feel my fingers.

Tingling in my hands.

Handcuffs so tight.

Muscly Alex lifts me to my feet.

I'm wobbly.

'You're a big man.'

I laugh.

'You gotta learn to do what you're told, boy,' Alex says, his words like knives in my ear. 'You blackfellas never learn.'

My cheek against the wall.

Feels like my cheek shatters on impact.

Blood in my mouth.

Tastes all metally.

White wall.

Breathe.

In

And

Out.

In

And

Out.

When Trey was thirteen and I was seven, we readied our bikes in Aunty Dawn's backyard. It was a hot summer day and my helmet was loose on my head. Trey came to me and took his hands to the strap. He tightened it under my chin.

'Ow,' I said.

'Don't wanna give you no more brain damage,' Trey said to me, this cheeky smile on his face.

We rode our bikes to the top of the hill above the Valley, then we sped back down towards the T-intersection. The air blew through me. I wanted to stretch out my arms like I was flying, but I was too scared to let go of the handlebars. 'You're going too fast!' Trey shouted, but I could barely hear him over the wind rushing by my ears.

I pulled on my brake lever, but for some reason it wasn't working. I pulled on the lever again, and still nothing. I was only going faster. The T-intersection was growing closer and closer. A car drove past the intersection at the bottom of the hill. I lowered my feet from the pedals to the road and dragged my shoes along the bitumen to slow myself down, but I was still going too fast. Nothing was working. I was gonna have to jump.

Then, Trey banged into my side and I hit the road elbow first. There was an explosion of heat and a stabbing in my arm and then my leg. My skin began to sting immediately and my bike rattled as I slid down the road, coming to a stop just before the T-intersection.

I screamed so loud, I'm sure Mum and Dad could've heard me, wherever they were. Up the hill, I saw Trey getting up off the road. He examined his elbows and knees, and he was bleeding all over his thigh. He started running down to me. I tried to pull my leg out from under my bike, but the pain burst like a strike of lightning. My leg was purple and red. I screamed louder. I cried and my eyes were stinging by the time Trey got to me.

'You all right?' Trey asked.

'No!' I shouted.

'Shh. Calm down,' Trey said. I didn't stop crying, but I stopped screaming. Trey lifted the bike off my leg and moved it onto the grass.

'We need an ambulance,' I said.

'Ambulance? No way. Come on,' he said, crouching beside me with his back next to my body.

'What?'

'Climb on,' he said. 'I'll carry you home.'

'I'm dying!' I shouted. 'You need to call an ambulance!'

'I can't, Jamie. Now climb on.'

I took a deep breath, then lifted my arms to his shoulders and hauled myself on. The pain grew more intense as Trey stood and brought me up with him. He grabbed my good leg and held it by his side, then carried me all the way home to Aunty Dawn's house.

20

Last night is a blur. The back of my head has been throbbing ever since I woke up this morning back in Segro.

The psych has come to see me. She's propped her little plastic chair on the other side of my door and I'm just standing there.

'Jamie, do you want to talk about what happened last night?' she asks.

'He had it comin'.'

'What do you mean?'

'That screw was talking shit while I was trying to chill with my mate,' I say. 'He was talking to me like I was a baby, telling me it was my bedtime.'

'Why was he saying it was your bedtime?' she asks.

'Because we'd finished dinner, and it was time to go to our rooms. But that's not the point.'

I'm pacing back and forth at my door.

'Who were you talking to?'

'Well, that's hardly any of your business, miss.'

'So, you hit him because he was telling you to go to bed *when* it was time for bed?'

'He hit me too! He's been trying to work me up since I got in here. He was asking for it. He should know better than to talk to us like we're babies. It's his own fault.' I'm shouting and my throat is sore. I need to chill.

Deep breath.

'I had a bad moment,' I say.

'Last time you had a bad moment, you caused a big fight and ended up on the roof for six hours,' she says.

'Yesssss, but that was a completely different situation.'

She pencils something into the notepad she's got resting on her knees.

'Do you think you might have difficulties with your anger?' she asks.

'What?' I sigh. 'Here we go, being analysed about stupid shit. It's not about my anger,' I say. 'It's about these screws thinking they got all the power over us.'

The psych pencils something down again.

'I want to try some breathing techniques with you,' she says. 'They'll help you control your anger better.'

'No, thank you,' I say. 'I can breathe just fine, been doing it my whole life.'

I'm bored with this whole thing, so I just go and lie on my bed and stay quiet. A few minutes pass before she finally gives up and leaves with her chair.

I stay in bed until lunch. The screws bring me a ham sandwich with just sliced ham and bread, no butter or salad or anything else. It's a pretty shitty lunch. As I finish eating,

Shae comes to my room. She lets herself in and picks up a small piece of paper from the floor.

'What's this?' she asks. I realise it's the paper with Oodgeroo Noonuccal's poem.

'Nothing,' I say. 'I don't know.'

'Oh, this is a good poem,' Shae says. She locks the door and sits down at the end of my bed. I want to tell her to fuck off because I'm still angry she was trying to guilt me into changing my mind about seeing my dad. 'The first poems I ever liked were by Oodgeroo Noonuccal. She had a way of really saying what needed to be said.'

'Yeah?'

'This one, though…' she says. 'Where'd you get this?'

'It was in one of the poetry books in the library.'

'Why'd you take it?'

I'm feeling all nervous for some reason. I know I'm not in trouble because Shae's not angry or anything.

'I dunno,' I say. 'I wanted to read it properly.'

'And what did you think?'

'Umm.' I rest back against the wall. 'It was cool. It was very strong, if you know what I mean. But it was also sad.'

Shae nods. 'Do you like poetry?'

'Yeah, I guess. But not in like a *nerdy* way or anything.'

'So do I,' Shae says. 'Not in a *nerdy* way either. But you know, all this stuff with your brother and your parents, you probably don't like talking about it, right? Poetry is a way you can put it into words. It's all about how you feel. It's about expressing what's in here.' Shae points to her chest and I am about to crack up laughing.

'Rightio.'

'How about we do something? I'll write a poem and you write a poem, then we'll sit down and read them together. You wanna?'

I giggle. It honestly sounds absurd, but Shae isn't giggling like I am.

'You're serious?' I ask.

'Yeah, why not?'

She's daring me. She reckons I'll back down.

'Okay, let's do it,' I say.

'I'll come back in a week,' she says, before she leaves with a great big smile on her face.

While I'm out for my rec time, the screws let me use a pencil and paper, still in handcuffs. That's when I realise I don't know how the fuck to write a poem. I think about what Shae said: *It's all about how you feel. It's about expressing what's in here.*

How I feel. How I feel. How I feel.

I feel regret. I feel loss. I could write a poem about Mum and Dad. I could write about how I feel about them. Shae would know then, though. I don't know if *I* want *her* to know all that.

Something else. Something else I feel.

I sit up on the tabletop and plant my feet on the seat. The table is hard on my arse – it's like sitting on the hardest rock on earth. It's kind of like a picnic table, I guess, except made of metal instead of wood.

I remember sitting on a *wooden* picnic table just like this one. I was little. I could smell sea water, and there was a

182

team of seagulls surrounding me. It was the day before me and Trey were taken. Aunty Dawn took us in and had to change her whole life for us. She did this really amazing thing for us.

I feel guilt – guilt for what I've done to Aunty Dawn and Uncle Bobby. They're now the carers of a good-for-nothing-high-risk-offender-waste-of-space criminal, who steals cars and runs from the police. The white people in town will scoff and shake their heads when they see Aunty Dawn walking through the supermarket, filling her trolley with groceries. *There's Jamie Langton's aunty. She's such a failure,* they'll whisper to each other, quiet enough to feel safe to say it, but loud enough for Aunty Dawn to hear.

The words are flaring in my head. They're all there suddenly and my fingers race to jot them down.

I was sitting at a wooden picnic table with Trey and we were munching away at chips which rested on butcher's paper on the table. Behind Trey's shoulders, I could see the river mouth. I had chicken salt on my lips and I licked them, while Trey shooed away the seagulls that were on the ground, waiting for us to throw them a chip.

'They're fucking coming to the house tomorrow,' Mum shouted at Dad as they stood beside our car. 'Why didn't you fucking shower the boys? If they take my boys from me—'

'What the fuck do you want me to do?' Dad shouted back.

Me and Trey were quiet, and they just kept yelling and yelling. Mum's voice became hoarse and she started crying.

I looked over to them, confused. I was worried me and Trey might eat all the chips and they would miss out because of their arguing.

'Just eat,' Trey whispered to me, when he caught me staring over to Mum and Dad. 'Just eat.'

I wasn't feeling hungry, but I brought the chips to my mouth. The salt tingled at the corners of my lips as I looked down to the seagulls beside us. They were begging us for a chip, so I threw one at them and they all raced for it like they were about to starve to death.

21

I keep track of the days in Segro by marking them on the wall with a stroke of my fingernail into the soft concrete. It's day nine of my second stint in Segro. As I lie on my bed, I find myself remembering a song Aunty Dawn played by Archie Roach, loud as she could from the speakers: 'F Troop'. He sang about meeting his brother and going into a spiral of drinking and bumming around, but it was all okay because he had a brother now. It kind of feels like how it is with me and Trey – like I've been getting to know my brother all over again. I feel like all that frustration I had with him is fading away.

Shae appears at my door and I realise it's poetry-reading-out-loud day. The screws let me out of my room, but my handcuffs stay on. I sit with Shae at the edge of the courtyard. She unfolds her poem and places it flat on the table. I'm suddenly feeling all nervous. I wasn't before, but now that I'm about to read my poem out loud, I'm shaking in my shoes.

'You wanna go first?' Shae asks.

'Nah.'

'You sure you don't want to just get it out of the way?'

'You first, I reckon.'

Shae takes a deep breath, looking over the scribbly writing on the paper, then clears her throat.

'It was a cold day.

When the bird left its nest. Gone.

Never to return.'

She looks up to me and smiles.

'What? Was that it?' I ask.

'Yeah. It's a haiku. They're only short.'

'But I wrote a longer one.'

'So read it,' she says, folding her arms on the table.

'You just did a simple one, so it won't be a fair game.'

'It's not a game,' Shae says. 'It's *poetry*. Let's hear it.'

I take my own piece of paper from my pocket, look over the words I've written. My handwriting is shit and I think this is the first time I'm realising that. I take a breath, same as Shae did.

'Mother. Aunty.

Carer. Protector.

Watcher. Guardian.

Her hair is curly.

A short woman with lines

On her face.

Small brown hands,

The hands she used to pick him up.

Broken child.

Hands lifted the child, small child,
To his feet.
Taught him to stand.
To run, to smile.
His small brown hands he placed in hers.
Aunty's hands.
Mother's hands.
The broken child she raised,
Falls
Over and over.
He falls and reaches for her.
Aunty. Mother.
Her grip finds his skinny wrist.
She pulls him from the dark place
And brings him home.
Sorry, he says.
I'm sorry you were the one I needed.
Watcher. Guardian.
Carer. Protector.
Mother. Aunty.
Mother.'

When I finish reading the poem, Shae's looking at me funny. Her eyebrows are in some demented shape and her mouth has pinched at the centre.

'I kind of wrote it the same way Oodgeroo Noonuccal wrote her poem, you know, without the rhyming and that.'

'Jamie, you clever boy,' she says.

I can't help but feel this strange warmness fill my body. My cheeks are red, I'm sure. Shae smiles when she looks at me. It's kind of awkward, so I look away, but I think she must see something else in me – kind of the same way Mr Barrett reckons he sees something in me. I don't know what it is, but maybe I'm beginning to see something too.

22

It's December-something – it's so hard to keep track of it when you're in Segro. Another week has gone by and my sentencing day has arrived. I haven't seen Alex around since our fight. Maybe he got fired like he deserved to be.

I have a quick shower and dress in my black polo shirt and trackpants. I don't brush my teeth, because I can't be bothered putting all that effort into making my breath smell good when I'm just going to be sitting in front of a screen.

The screws arrive at my door in Segro, handcuffs at the ready. All cuffed-up, they escort me through the locked doors and the corridors and the walkways. We come to the office building and they take me into the video room. I sit down and stare at the black screen for a moment. I see myself reflected back. My hair has gotten so much longer since I've been in here. Using my fingers, I brush it to the side and behind my ears as best I can.

'They'll be up in a minute,' the screw says, sitting behind

me in the corner of the room. I just rest back on my chair and wait.

Ten minutes passes by.

Fifteen.

Finally, the screen lights up and I see the courtroom. The magistrate sits up at her bench in her stupid black robe. My lawyer is Trudy again. She sits with the bulldog-woman at their long table, sharing whispers and jotting things down on their papers in front of them. Behind them in the audience is an old white lady and another younger-looking girl. I wish Aunty Dawn or Trey were somewhere in the seats. It's just me and the white people. The judge starts to talk and I decide I'd better sit upright. The lawyers look up at me.

'James, can you hear us?' the magistrate asks.

'Yes,' I say.

The magistrate starts to talk legal lingo, then the lawyers do the same. It's like listening to Russian people speaking to one another. How the hell am I supposed to understand anything? My brain is small enough. How can they expect me to follow any of this?

'Danger to the community...'

That, I understand. It's all the same shit they say, over and over again.

'High risk of reoffending...'

'Bad influence on his peers...'

'Childhood trauma...'

'Concerns about decline in mental health...'

'Lack of cultural support...'

My head is aching with the noise of their voices coming through the speakers. I just want to go to sleep, but then the magistrate says we will come back after lunch for the sentencing.

During lunch, I'm sat in a waiting area. Another boy is in here for AVL, and we are both handcuffed. The screws have brought us a bucket of apples, so we are both eating one. I'm not really hungry, but my throat is dry and I figure I can get some juice from the apple.

The screws take me back into the video room and sit me down. The cuffs come off and I stare once more at the black screen. A few minutes pass and nothing has happened, so I rest my head on the table. The table is hard and cold, thick plastic. I want to just bash my head into it. Maybe I'll slip into a coma and sleep out my sentence.

The screen lights up again and the courtroom comes back. The old white lady and the young white girl are still sitting in the audience section. The magistrate and the lawyers pick up right where they left off – going on and on again in their legal lingo.

The magistrate says something that sounds like *take and drive*, then something that sounds like *property damage*. She says the sum of the damage and it is over twenty thousand dollars. I reckon Mark Cassidy could afford it, though.

'Significant property damage to the roof at Kinston,' the judge says.

It seems like this list is going on forever. Then she turns to me for a moment, telling me she has come to an appropriate sentence.

She lists off the offences again, but this time, she adds the words *control order.*

'Ten months,' she says. 'Five months...control order, starting August twentieth...Five months...good behaviour bond...'

The magistrate thanks me for being patient and the screen turns to black again. I'm not sure I can fully comprehend what's just happened. When I get back to Segro, the screws tell me my legal aid is on the phone.

'How are you feeling?' Trudy asks. 'Good outcome, yeah?'

'Good?'

'You've only got one month left. You're serving a five-month sentence in custody, starting from the day you were arrested. You're being released on January twentieth.'

I don't know how the hell I missed that – I guess I'm dumber than I thought. I'm being released in January – one month to go.

Back in my room, I go to my dirty clothes, search through my shorts. In the pockets, I find the Oodgeroo Noonuccal poem. I sit on my bed and read it over and over and over until I'm calm. I consume the words, replay them in a deeper voice in my head.

One month to go. One month.

23

It's Christmas Day and the screws bring me and Ronnie out of our rooms in Segro.

Screws in riot gear handcuff us and take us to one of the classrooms and I see the block letters written across the whiteboard in red, black and yellow:

KOORI CHRISTMAS.

There's a table with sliced fruit and sandwiches and juice. A tall Christmas tree is stashed in the corner, decorated in tinsel and fake snow, which is hilarious to me because it's like thirty-nine degrees today. Shae and some of the other youth workers are in the room, along with some Kooris wearing work polos with Aboriginal designs and their organisation's symbol on them.

Aside from me and Ronnie, there are six other Koori kids. One wears a purple polo. Two of the others must be new because they're wearing the white polos from the Induction Unit, and the other two are wearing red. One is wearing a green polo and I walk over to him.

'What's your name, cuz?' I ask. 'I'm Jamie.'

'Lochlan,' he says.

'Do you know someone named Lenny? He was in your unit last I saw him.'

'Lenny? Yeah, he got out a few weeks ago,' Lochlan says.

'Oh.'

Shae calls for our attention. She says an acknowledgement of country then tells us the names of all external visitors who are here and the services they work for.

'Make sure you have a yarn to these fullas when we have a feed, but first, come and grab a present each,' Shae says.

The boys start for the Christmas tree and I follow them. The presents are all wrapped in paper covered with pictures of Santa on his sleigh with the reindeer pulling him along. I reach for a present, but Shae stops me.

'Wait. This one's yours,' Shae says, pointing to the small rectangular one by the trunk of the tree. I unwrap it. I'm surprised when I peel the paper away, because it's the book of poetry I picked off the shelf when Shae had me and Ryan help her get books for the reading group: *Lemons in the Chicken Wire* by Alison Whittaker. I cover it back up when I see Ronnie, holding his unwrapped face cloth and socks, glancing over to me.

'Cool,' I say.

'Don't you want to have a look inside?' Shae asks.

'Nah, it's all good. I'll look at it later. Thanks.'

'No worries,' Shae says. 'How about I pop it in your property and you can have a look at it when you get out next month?'

'Sounds good,' I say, handing it to Shae.

I feel bad for not showing Shae how excited I really am, but I know the other boys will make fun of me if they see me reading a book of poetry.

We all head for the food. I grab a paper plate and load it with strawberries and mandarin and watermelon. I pour myself a paper cup of orange juice and take a sip. I could talk to one of the Aboriginal workers, but I notice Ronnie's sitting chewing away at a sandwich, all by himself. I head over and sit in the seat beside him.

Ronnie doesn't tell me to fuck off or anything, so I start eating my strawberries. Ronnie finishes his sandwiches and moves on to a piece of watermelon. As I take a sip from my cup of juice, I look over the rest of the people. The boys are talking to the external visitors, each of them with a different person. Shae is talking to one of them as well. Lochlan from the Green Unit is having a laugh, like he's catching up with an old friend.

'I'm getting out next month,' I say to Ronnie. I won't tell him, but I'm kind of scared to go home and see Aunty Dawn. I really need to make it up to her for getting locked up.

'I'm getting out in five days,' Ronnie says. 'Right in time for new year's.'

'Reckon you'll be back in here soon?' I ask. 'Free food, free bed and all that?'

'I dunno,' Ronnie says. 'If it goes to shit like I reckon it will. Spent more time in here than at home anyway.'

'Might be all right on the outside,' I say.

'Doubt it. I shouldn't stay out, anyway. I'm a *danger to the community*.'

'Me too, apparently.' I giggle.

195

I finish off my fruit and my juice and Ronnie finishes his feed as well.

'What were youse doin' the other day?' Ronnie asks. 'When Shae came into Segro and youse were sittin' at the table.' I feel nervous suddenly. 'Sounded like youse were readin' stories to each other.'

'Yeah.' I sigh.

'That's gay as.'

I want to say something, punch his face in, but instead I just stand and walk back to the table, load some more strawberries onto my plate.

After Koori Christmas, the screws in the riot gear take me and Ronnie back to Segro. They lock me in my room and I look across the courtyard to Ronnie's room.

This place is shit. This place is Ronnie, and Ronnie is this place. I don't want to be like Ronnie. No way. I don't want this place to be my home. Like a switch flicking in my head, I decide I ain't ever getting locked up again.

When I get back to the unit, I head to the phone. I call Aunty Dawn.

'Merry Christmas, Jamie-baby,' she says.

'You too, Aunt. What did you and Uncle Bobby get up to?'

'Oh, not much. We're just having Christmas dinner at home. Thought we'd have a quiet one this year. I've been a bit unwell, son. I'm sorry we haven't gotten up there to see you.'

'It's okay, Aunt. I'm out next month. I'll be right.'

'Good, good.'

'I was wondering...' I say. Nervousness comes to my stomach. 'Could you text Mum? Tell her I said to say *merry Christmas* to her and Dad?'

'Of course,' Aunty Dawn says. 'I'll text her right now. Thanks for calling. I love you.'

'Love you too, Aunt.'

I hang up and head to my room.

III

Trey comes in for a visit on the day after Christmas. He says he's sorry that all the timeslots were booked out for Christmas Day visits. I don't mind, though.

'Do they give youse anything in there for Christmas?' Trey asks.

'Most of the boys got some socks and undies,' I say. 'But I got a book. It's in my property, so I can read it when I get out. They put on a mad feed, too.'

'What kind of book is it?'

'It's just a book,' I say, feeling nervous suddenly. 'Jeez, so many questions.'

'Just askin'.' Trey smiles.

'You do anything for Christmas?'

'I spent it with Jacob at his parents' place. I was glad to get out of there though so I could come visit ya.'

'So, I'm just an excuse for you to get away?' I tease.

'Exactly. But I'm actually here, aren't I?'

'I guess.'

Trey's eyes widen like he's just been struck by lightning.

'I forgot to tell you,' he says. 'I found an old photo album when I was going through my stuff. It's just a pocket-sized thing, but there are pictures of us when we were kids with Mum and Dad. We look really happy in them.'

He leans forward and smiles, bringing something from his pocket: a small square photo of me and him, each of us sitting on one of Santa's knees. I'm a crying baby and Trey has a terrible bowl cut.

'Look how little we were. Finding the album brought back a lot of memories. I've got so many stories to tell ya, about Mum and Dad.'

I smile as I look over the photo, then the tears are rising to my eyes and the lump is returning to my throat.

'What's wrong?' Trey asks. I guess he's gotten used to reading me now.

'This photo was from when we were still together. We were still a family then.'

'Well, we're still family now,' Trey says. 'Even though we aren't together, we're still family.'

'I do miss them,' I say, sniffling back my tears.

After the visit, I head back to my room. Night comes. The lights come on outside and I lie in bed. The lads creep back into my mind. I push them away, try to think about the day the white people came into our house with the coppers and took us away from Mum and Dad. I don't know why I can't remember it happening. I close my eyes, try to form the images in my head. There's so much about that day I can't remember. It's like my brain has deleted it. I force myself to think harder.

A sniffle.

A car door closing.

A white man and a white woman, both wearing suits.

A cop outside my window.

Trey was crying when the cop forced him into the car. I was already in the back seat and my eyes were stinging too. My nose was runny and I wiped it on my shirt. Trey didn't even put on his seatbelt. He cried harder, covering his face with his hands.

I looked out the window. The cop was standing on the other side of the glass with his back to me. I leaned forward and looked back to our house. There were two people, a man and a woman, both wearing black suits. They stood beside another cop on the verandah, behind wooden posts and railings at the front of our little house. Dad was standing there, wiping tears from his face while he talked to them. Mum was lying on the ground beside Dad's feet. I tried to listen, but I couldn't hear what they were saying.

'Where are we going?' I asked Trey. He didn't answer me, so I turned back to the window. I could see our next-door neighbours standing on their verandah, looking over to the cop and the suited people and Mum and Dad

The cop on the verandah stayed there with Mum and Dad, but the suited people started for the car. They climbed into the front and then started the car.

'Where are we going?' I asked them.

'Shut up,' Trey said. He grabbed my arm and squeezed it so hard I thought he might break my wrist. 'Don't talk.'

'We're going to your aunty Dawn's house,' the woman in the front said.

As we began to drive away, Mum screamed, and her scream blasted through the glass of the car windows. I tried to look back to her and Dad, but we drove away too fast – all I managed to see was the cop standing on the lawn out the front of our house.

Trey sniffled back his tears as we drove and the outside of the car was a blur, like an oil painting. When we stopped driving, the suited man and woman got out and opened our doors. They walked us along the dirt to the stairs and up to the verandah, where Aunty Dawn and Uncle Bobby were waiting for us.

'Come here,' Aunty Dawn said. She wasn't so familiar to me then, but I hugged her anyway, and so did Trey. I cried into her shirt and she held me tighter.

24

It's January twentieth – my release day. I wake to banging at my door and the morning light shining through my window.

'Up ya get, Langton,' the screw says.

I get straight out of bed and into the shower. The water is cold against my skin and perks me right up. Today is the day I leave Kinston. It is my last day at Kinston EVER. I swear to myself that I'll never be back behind these concrete walls again.

My fingernails have gotten a bit long. Alongside all the days I've marked on the wall to keep track of the date, I use my fingernail to scratch my initials above my pillow: *JL was ere.*

I'm watching the sun move in the sky and waiting for the hours to tick over. I think to myself:

No more.

You are not coming back in here.

Get your life on track.

Maybe those are Trey's words filling my head. I haven't even been able to see Ryan, because I've been in Segro ever since I whacked Alex. I hope he's all right. He has his problems, and it does make me worry sometimes, when I'm just in my bed thinking about stuff. He hasn't come into Segro, though, so I guess he must be doing okay.

After I finish my bowl of cornflakes, Shae comes to my room. She unlocks the door and steps inside.

'Your brother is picking you up at twelve,' she says.

She unfolds a piece of paper she's holding and hands it to me.

'What's this?' I ask.

'It's a poem, one of my favourites.'

'"Daddy", by Sylvia Plath.'

I skim over the first section.

'If you don't know anything about Sylvia Plath yet, you should definitely do some research when you get out. She was this brilliant poet from the mid nineteen-hundreds. I don't know why, but her poems really speak to me.'

'*Speak* to you?'

'Yeah. I think that's why poetry exists,' Shae says. 'I think it's a way for us to express what's happening inside, how we observe things and how things affect us. It's a way for us to process things. We put it into poetry because it's easier than telling the truth or our story in plain words. It's like a song, and it speaks more to your heart than your brain.'

'I don't think we should do this,' I say, remembering how Ronnie said poetry was *gay*. 'Not right now, anyway.'

'You've got a voice inside you, Jamie,' Shae says. 'After hearing your poem, I think poetry might be the way for you to let that voice speak louder.'

'Right.'

'Anyway, read "Daddy". Sylvia Plath is talking about her father, who died when she was a child. The way she basically blasts him with the full force of her heart is really powerful.'

'The *full force of her heart*?' I chuckle.

Shae takes the paper back and reads the poem out loud. As she speaks, I think I'm starting to see what she's talking about. This poem is powerful, all right. By the time Shae finishes reading, I'm sure I love it.

Two screws come through the gate and into Segro. They head for my room and open the door.

'Time to go, Langton,' one of the screws says.

'Excited?' Shae asks as I follow her out of my room.

'I guess so,' I say. But I don't know if I'm excited. Maybe I'm a little scared. I'm scared I'll fuck up again, and just like that, I'll be back in Kinston or somewhere else. I'm worried the lads will cut my throat as soon as I set foot back in DB.

I walk with Shae and the screw through the locked doors and to the admin desk. Shae retrieves my property bag, which contains the clothes I wore when I came in, my dead phone and *Lemons in the Chicken Wire*. They are all just sitting in the plastic bag. We walk back through the white-walled corridors and I follow Shae into the garage. She rambles on about keeping out of trouble and making positive friends and finding something to do to keep me busy. As the garage door rolls up, I see Trey rushing to stomp a cigarette out under his shoe.

Shae offers me a handshake. 'Now, you stay out of trouble, hey? All decisions lead somewhere. Don't let the wrong decision lead you back in here.'

'I'll try,' I say, giving her a smile. 'And thanks for the book. I promise I'll start reading it right away. And tell Ryan I said to look after himself? I didn't get to say goodbye.'

'I will,' Shae says. 'Good luck, Jamie.'

I give Shae a nod. I start walking away, then stop.

'You told me a while ago that we only get one mum and one dad,' I say to Shae.

'I did.'

'But you were wrong. I got two mums and two dads, because I've got my Aunty Dawn and Uncle Bobby too.'

Shae smiles at me and I smile back. I head over to Trey, who also shakes my hand. I follow him to his little black Toyota Corolla and get in.

I'm feeling good as we drive out of the car park. A sense of déjà vu comes over me, and some deep, hidden worry surfaces that this doesn't feel like the last time I will drive out of the Kinston car park.

'You could've just put me on the bus,' I say. 'It's only a couple of hours down the coast.'

'No worries. It's a decent drive and besides, it'll be nice to see the old people for a couple of days.'

Trey's got a real fresh haircut today. It's trimmed, faded on the sides and back. He isn't a big fan, though, saying that the barber cut it shorter than he wanted.

We pull into the Maccas car park across the highway. I get us a table as Trey orders our food. He comes back with a large McChicken meal for me and for himself, large chips and a cappuccino. I bite right into the McChicken and let the taste of the chicken and mayo relax onto my tongue.

'We could see the Maccas sign from the roof of the juvie when we were up there,' I say, taking another bite. 'It was like it was just sitting over here teasing us.'

Trey takes a sip from his coffee and smiles.

'Do you remember when we first started living with Aunty Dawn and Uncle Bobby? We were playin' up a lot, so they took us on a road trip to Newcastle for the weekend. We stopped at that Maccas in the middle of nowhere.'

I nearly choke on my McChicken.

'Yes,' I say. 'And those fullas that were dressed like cowboys in the car park. Boots, jeans, cowboy hats.'

'Uncle Bobby said to them, *youse are a long way from the ranch.*'

'Yes! And then they got angry and one of 'em tried to get Uncle Bobby to fight them, and Uncle Bobby said, *I don't fight white trash.*'

We both laugh so hard there at our table inside the Maccas. My lungs are sore by the time I finish laughing, and Trey's face is all red and his eyes are watering. As he catches his breath, Trey sighs.

'Did you know I hated them at first?' he asks. I shake my head. 'Uncle Bobby and Aunty Dawn. I thought they were trying to replace Mum and Dad as our parents. It wasn't until I got older and moved away that I realised they were just trying to give us a good life. They did their best.'

I just nod. I finish my Maccas and then we get back in the car. Trey starts playing some Eminem from his stereo as we get on the highway.

'Three hours to go,' I say.

'Three hours.'

We head out of town and follow the highway alongside the coastline, and I look out to the white shores and infinite ocean knowing I'm heading home to Dalton's Bay, where Mark Cassidy and the footy heads are waiting.

PART 3
THE MAN

25

The sun is setting in Dalton's Bay as we cross the bridge over the harbour and into town. I'm dreading seeing Mark Cassidy and the lads. As we pass through town, there seems to be less people around. Somehow it feels like the town has changed colours.

'It's weird being here,' Trey says.

'Yeah?'

'Didn't think I'd be back so soon.'

'Soon? It's been like three years.' I giggle.

'Three years ain't that long.'

Sergeant Hudson and Constable Minelli are at the café opposite the youth centre, sitting at a round table off the footpath.

'Wanna swing by the *old place*?' Trey asks as we drive past.

We head over the hill to the Valley, passing by Lenny's old house. It's got a Tongan flag in the window now. Dally's house looks quiet. I wonder if he is out of juvie yet.

We pass the block of units where Georgia lives. I haven't thought of her in ages. There's an old Koori fulla out front, probably around fifty, smoking a cigarette against the gate to the property. He's got curly black hair and a greying beard. It's weird because I don't know who he is, and I thought I knew everyone in the Valley.

'I remember why I left, now,' Trey says. 'Look at how shit this place is.'

He drives on through the Valley. We pass a park with a swing set and a slide in the middle of it, though the equipment is mostly hidden by the long grass.

Trey turns into a cul-de-sac and stops out the front of a little blue house – the blue paint has faded and now it's more grey.

'Here we are,' he says. 'Our old house.'

I gaze over the lawn – patchy grass and children's toys.

'It looks different from how I remember it.'

I gaze over the four steps which lead up to the verandah with wooden posts and railings. Two chairs rest on either side of a small round table.

'Those are the stairs, right? The ones I fell down and hit my head,' I say.

'Yep,' Trey says. 'That's where the Humpty Dumpty thing began.'

I remember falling down the stairs, the hard concrete. Mum was leaning on the railing with her elbows and I was swinging back and forth on the handrail. I slipped and Mum tried to catch my shorts, but I still fell. She yelled at me and I cried, then she hugged me.

The front door opens and a young woman comes out carrying a baby on her hip. She rushes down the stairs to the little Ford in the driveway.

She fixes her baby in the car seat. She spots us. I give her a wave and she waves back, narrowing her eyes. It's pretty funny really – she's just come out of her house and seen these two Aboriginal guys parked out the front staring at her yard and house.

Trey drives around the block, past the streetlight and into the bush to Aunty Dawn's house. We pull up beside Uncle Bobby's ute.

The air is warm when I get out of the car. We get our bags and Uncle Bobby meets us at the front door. He greets Trey with a hug. Uncle Bobby squeezes him tight, closes his eyes.

'Good to see ya, son,' he says.

'You too, Unk.'

He lets Trey inside and gives me a hug too.

'Welcome back, Jamie,' he says, before he lets me go.

Inside, Aunty Dawn is sitting on the couch with her feet up on the ottoman. The telly's on and she's watching *The Chase*. Trey places his duffel bag on the floor and goes to Aunty Dawn. He leans down and hugs her. Her arms rise to his back and she holds him tighter.

'*Trey-Trey*,' she whispers. When she lets Trey go, she holds his face up to hers with her hands on both his cheeks. 'You're so handsome.'

Uncle Bobby heads to the kitchen. 'You want a cuppa, Trey?' he calls out.

'Yeah, just a coffee, thanks, Unk. Milk and two sugars.'

'You, Jamie?'

'Nah, I'm right.'

Aunty Dawn stands from the couch and opens her arms. I walk into her embrace and we hug. It's a warm, tight cuddle.

'You've put on some weight,' Aunty Dawn says. I laugh quietly into her shoulder. 'Good to have you back, son.'

My bedroom is exactly as I left it, except my bed is made, the blankets tucked in at the corners. My phone charger is still plugged into the wall. I connect my phone and when it powers up, the texts start coming through – messages from Andy, Stevie and the other boys, counting down the days, saying they miss me, that they want to catch up when I'm out. But there are also messages from Mark Cassidy.

You're dead.

I'm gonna fuck you up when I see you again.

Every dog has his day.

UR fucked. I'm gonna cut your throat. Why don't you kill urself and save me the trouble.

I swallow, stop reading. My heart is racing. I kick off my shoes and lie on my bed.

I send a group text to Dally and Lenny:

Everyone out?

I pull out the book Shae gave me – *Lemons in the Chicken Wire*. The scrap of paper falls out with the poem I wrote for Aunty Dawn. Shae didn't bin it. I guess she kept it for a while, then decided to give it back to me.

I pick up the poem and read over it again. It's good, I think. It's poetry. It's embarrassing. I slide it back into the book, keep it hidden in the pages, then place the book on my bookshelf in front of one of my Goosebumps books: *The Knight in Screaming Armour.*

Trey comes to my doorway, holding his cup of coffee in one hand and his duffel bag in the other.

'You right?' he asks, placing his bag against my wall.

'Yeah. All good,' I say. 'You're not sleeping in here, are you?'

'Chill out, I'll be in my old room with all the boxes.' He walks to the bathroom next door and I hear him turn on the shower. The rushing water is still loud in the walls of my bedroom as it travels the pipes.

The sun sets and we all sit down at the table for dinner. Time is flying today.

Aunty Dawn dishes out a roasted pork breast with crackling and roast potatoes, carrots and pumpkin on the side. Uncle Bobby mixes the instant gravy by the kettle and brings it over to the table in a bowl.

'So, how was it, Jamie? Were the boys rough on ya?' Uncle Bobby asks.

I use my knife and fork and cut my pork into smaller pieces.

'Nah,' I say. 'It wasn't like that. It was just...shit.'

I pour the gravy over my pork and bring a piece onto my tongue. It's like a firework of flavour in my mouth and I'm sure it's the best thing I've ever tasted.

'You're a strong boy,' Aunty Dawn says. 'You need to be strong enough to not end up back in there.'

'I won't,' I say. Trey smiles at me when I say that, as he chews his first mouthful.

After dinner, Trey gets a fire started in the firepit out the front. Uncle Bobby sets up some chairs in a circle so we can all sit out there. Aunty Dawn heads straight to bed, though.

I'm stuffed from dinner. The fire flickers and it's almost hypnotising to just watch it burn, to watch the smoke billow to the sky. I could fall asleep right here.

'I thought I hated Dalton's Bay, but I really missed this place,' Trey says. 'It's truly beautiful.'

'What are you? A real estate agent or something?' I tease.

'You know what I mean,' Trey says.

Uncle Bobby heads inside and comes back out with two beers. He hands one to Trey.

'Your father been in touch with ya?' Uncle Bobby asks Trey.

'Yeah, I went up and visited them. Jamie's not keen on it, though.'

'Mmm.' Uncle Bobby sits down beside me. 'Your dad was a good man when you fullas were kids,' he says to me. 'He and your mum really loved you boys. They was always fighting to get youse back.'

'Then they stopped,' I say.

'They didn't *stop*,' Uncle Bobby says. 'The system stopped them. Once you're on their books, they fuck you over and over and over.'

I scoff. Uncle Bobby turns to me.

'This *colonial* system is hard for us blackfullas to deal with,' he says. 'That's the way it was built and designed, so they always hold power over us, so that we can never win.

214

They reckon that the Stolen Generations ended years ago, but you boys are proof nothing ended. The white colonial system just found another way. It's a quieter way, now, but it's the same.'

Trey nods.

'Don't ever think your mother and father didn't try, because they did,' Uncle Bobby says.

We sit outside for a while longer. We're quiet. I'm mostly in my head, thinking over Uncle Bobby's words. Maybe Mum and Dad did fight for us. Maybe they did really try. Maybe it's not all their fault.

Around midnight, Uncle Bobby yawns. 'I'm headin' to bed. Don't stay out too much longer, ay?'

He takes his chair to the verandah where he leaves it, then he disappears inside.

'It's different for me too,' I say. 'It feels different being back here.'

'I've decided I'm gonna stick around for a week or two, relax a bit. I was wondering... have you thought about what I asked you when you were in juvie? About living with me and Jacob? I'll look after ya, get ya into a good school,' Trey says. His voice sounds different, deeper, like he's aged twenty years. 'I want us to be brothers again, you know? I've missed having your big head around.'

'I don't know.'

Trey sits forward. 'I know Aunty Dawn and Uncle Bobby would miss ya, but I feel like I've got a lot of time to make up for.'

'I got my mates here,' I say, shaking my head.

'Your *mates*.' Trey sighs. I know he reckons they're no good, but they're my boys. We've got each other's backs. We always have. It gets me thinking, though. I'm still thinking about it when I decide to call it a night and leave Trey sitting outside a little longer. Maybe I *could* move to Sydney, live with Trey. We would be a family again – at least half a family. I imagine waking up in the morning, getting dressed in my school uniform, then heading to the breakfast table. Trey and this Jacob lad would be there with a banquet of bacon and eggs on the table. I'd eat with them, then head off to school. Sydney would be a whole new world for me. I could be a whole new person there. I could be different, change who I am.

In bed, I open my phone and go to the group message I sent to Dally and Lenny. No replies yet, but Lenny's seen the message. He's seen it and he hasn't replied. He doesn't want to reply. I re-create his face in my mind, the look he gave me when I saw him at Kinston in the Green Unit. I imagine it's the look he wore when he saw a message appear on his phone with my name. He hates me. He wants nothing to do with me anymore. He'll never forgive me and Dally for that night.

26

I've been out of juvie for a week and now school's going back. The first day of school is a Friday for some reason. In the bathroom, I give my face a quick shave with one of my new razors.

'You know you'll have to shave all the time now,' Trey teases from the doorway.

'I don't care, I don't like the stubble I got goin' on. Makes me look ratty.'

I change into my school uniform and grab my backpack. I get in Trey's car and we drive to Andy's house. I'm stuck with Andy now, just as I feared.

'How's it goin', cuz?' he asks, as he gets into the back of Trey's car. He reaches to me for a handshake.

'Good, cuz.'

'Long time no see. How was lock-up? Musta been rough, ay? You prob'ly got mad fightin' skills now. Did you get in heaps of fights? Did anyone try to shiv ya?'

'No.' I sigh.

Like me, he's wearing grey pants and our senior shirts, which are red and white, because we are in Year Eleven now.

'Have a good one,' Trey says as we arrive at the school gates.

'Thanks,' me and Andy reply.

The school somehow looks fifty years older. As I follow Andy onto the grounds, I feel like everyone's looking at me.

Juvie-boy's come back to school.

At lunchtime, me and Andy walk onto the oval. Some groups of girls are sitting in circles on the grass. There are kids hanging out by the back fence, which is steel and black and tall. Some of the little Year Seveners are running around and chasing each other, playing tag or something.

We head for the group of kids getting ready to play touch footy. There are about twelve of them. Most of them are in senior uniforms, but there are a few juniors joining in.

'Porter,' Andy says, pointing to the tall muscly white kid with massive calves. 'He's still talking about playing NRL. Reckons their scouts have been lookin' at him. But he's still here in DB, isn't he?'

'Come on,' I say, leading Andy towards the game on the oval. 'Time to break the ice, I reckon.'

Me and Andy join the team versing Porter Davis. We kick off to them. I jog beside Andy as we move up and start playing. The tall teacher with a wide-brimmed hat on play-ground duty has his eyes on us. He's got his shirt tucked in, his blue tie fixed and his sleeves kept long to his wrists. He's probably remembering back when he had young legs and could play footy.

The ball lands in Andy's hands and he sprints ahead. I'm unfit as hell, but I race up in support and loop behind Andy, calling out his name. Andy 'Benji Marshall' flicks the ball back to me. I look for support to my right.

Skinny white kid running up.

BANG.

Elbow to my face.

Everything goes black.

I hit the grass hard.

My head is burning hot.

Blood rushes from my nose, raining all over my school shirt.

Standing over me is Porter Davis.

'What the fuck?'

'A taste of what's to come, juvie-boy,' Porter says.

I jump straight to my feet, dizzy. My fists are clenched. My fingernails dig into my palm. My nose is still bleeding. I grab Porter by the collar. He's taller than me. Bigger than me. I don't care.

Porter grabs my shirt as well. He shoves me back. He's strong – stronger than me. Andy's arm comes between us. He tries to push us apart, but our eyes are locked. Porter looks like a mad dog, straight out of hell. He wants to hit me as much as I want to hit him. But I don't just want to hit him, I want to kill him.

'Oi,' a deep voice calls out from somewhere behind us. A big hairy hand grips my arm and the other pushes on Porter's chest. 'Out of it!'

It's the tall teacher with the wide-brimmed hat.

'Let go, boys,' he says. I let go and so does Porter. My nose is still stinging and I lift my shirt up to it to stop the blood from rushing out of my nostrils.

'Sir, it was an accident,' Porter says as we head inside. *'Juvie-boy* just took it too seriously. He's got anger problems. And do you know him and his mates steal cars?'

'Enough, Porter,' the tall teacher says. Porter wants to kill me too – I can see it in his eyes. But then he just scoffs and turns around.

'Come on,' Andy says, grabbing me by the arm. He walks with me down to the front office and sits with me in the sick bay as I hold tissues up to my bleeding nose. My fist is still clenched when I sit down, but I let it rest. I'm hot and I can't shake this nervousness in my stomach.

The bell rings and Andy heads to class.

I stay in the sick bay until period six English, even though my nose stopped bleeding ages ago. I was excited to see Mr Barrett, but one of the PE teachers arrives instead.

'All right, everyone,' she says as we pack into the classroom. 'Mr Barrett's away, and I have a heap of assessment tasks to mark, so we're having a quiet reading class today.'

Everyone pulls out the books they've been reading. I should've packed my book of poetry.

My nose is still sore, but I head to the bookshelf. I scan the titles, settle for *The Absolutely True Diary of a Part-time Indian* by Sherman Alexie, and bring it back to my desk.

The book has got pictures on some pages and it's written so well. It tells the story of when the author was a kid in America. It's about his childhood, growing up on a reservation as a Native American. I get halfway through the book really quickly – too quickly. This is a good book and I don't want to finish it too fast. It makes me wonder what I would say if I was to write a book about my childhood one day. It would be a pretty depressing story, I reckon. Maybe it would be better as poetry. I get my English book from my pigeonhole below the whiteboard. I head back to my desk and take my pen to the next empty page. The words are flooding my brain – a poem about Shae. It's her voice in my head, bringing the words to me like fingers running through my hair.

I finish my poem as the final bell sounds, then set my English book back in the pigeonhole and take my bag.

After school, I head to the gates and turn to the road. A car drives into my view. It slows to a stop at the crossing. A sparkling new white Holden Trax.

Mark Cassidy's in the driver's seat, with Porter Davis in the passenger's, and three other lads bunched together in the back. Their biceps are big and muscly. They stare at me. They all hate me – Mark especially. He frowns at me, evil-eyed.

'Dead man walking,' Mark shouts as his frown turns into a slight smile, one that only a maniac would wear. Then he spins the tyres and speeds off through the crossing.

27

I don't want to go home. I could tell Trey about the threats, but he wouldn't take them seriously. He'd just laugh and tell me not to worry about it.

I walk to Stevie's house and knock on the door. There's gunfire blaring and I can hear Stevie and his cousin talking inside. I knock again, louder, and footsteps boom towards me.

'Jamie?' Stevie says, answering the door, eyes wide like I've startled him. 'You're out? Good to see ya. Sorry, we're just playing Modern Warfare II.' He opens the screen door for me. 'How was your first trip inside?'

'It was fine. But those lads are after me. Mark Cassidy wants to get me back for his car.' I'm almost breathless. I step inside Stevie's house and take a seat at the end of the couch.

'They're all talk,' Stevie says. 'We got your back, anyway. They gotta go through us first. They can't kill ya, obviously.'

'But what if they do?' I ask. 'What's to stop them from

killing me and dumping my body in DB Harbour? Who would care? The cops wouldn't.'

'Relax, bruh,' Stevie says, giggling to himself. He races up the hall and brings back a bong and some weed chopped up in a bowl. 'Just have a hit of this. Calm yourself down.'

'You're no help,' I say.

'Relax, Jamie brother,' Stevie says, slowly removing my backpack from by shoulders. 'Let's grab a charge and get the boys. You can stay the night if ya want. Don't worry 'bout those pricks.'

I don't argue. I go with Stevie in his Commodore into town. He heads into the bottle shop and comes out with two cases of beer.

The house is a party destination when we get back. Music is playing and Andy and the rest of the boys fill Stevie's lounge room. Stevie opens one of the cartons and we all flock to the beers like seagulls.

Stevie's mum and aunty are sitting at a small foldable table at the back door with half-drunk stubbies of VB in front of them. They are both smoking cigarettes and offer me a nod and a smile. Stevie's mum waves me over as I place some of the beers in the fridge.

'Jamie Langton,' Stevie's mum says. 'You've grown up. Seems like just yesterday you was in nappies.'

'I use the toilet these days, Aunt,' I say and she cracks up. The music changes and it's Archie Roach coming through the speakers. It's his song 'Took the Children Away'.

The women are singing along with it, but they don't sound too good.

'You know my Aunty Dawn?' I ask. 'She loves Archie Roach. She calls him the Godfather of Aboriginal music.'

'Yeah, we know old Aunty Dawn,' Stevie's mum says.

'The way she speaks about him and his songs is like nothing else,' I say. 'She truly loves him.'

I reach to the stereo and turn up the volume. I head back to the couch and take a seat. Listening to the music, thinking about how much Aunty Dawn loves Archie Roach, it makes me wonder if I could ever love something that much. I wonder if I could love *anything* that much. It also makes me wonder if anyone could ever love me that much. Could anyone?

I head back to the lounge room. The sounds of gunfire and shouting fill the room. Andy's on the old beaten couch playing Xbox with a few of the boys. I join them and Andy hands me his controller.

I sink my first beer with no real effort. This brand feels a lot smoother down the throat than any beer I've had before. And I'm so shit at Call of Duty tonight. I'm usually good, but I can't even land a head-shot right now.

I move on to my third beer and pass the controller to Andy, who's sitting on the floor now with his legs crossed.

'I'll text the girls, get them over,' Stevie says, whipping out his phone. I space out as I sit there watching the game being played on the telly.

The night goes on and I've lost count of how many beers I've had, but the first case is nearly empty. I'm not tired anymore, though. I'm not sad or anything really, just drunk. Stevie changes positions on the couch and sits beside me.

'We're going to meet up with the girls,' he says. 'They want us to go to theirs.' I don't protest. My feet are ready for an adventure, and I'm buzzing.

The boys all slip on their shoes and hoodies and we jostle out the front door. I'm wobbly on my feet for a moment, but as we pass under the streetlights, I begin to feel a little more balanced.

It's a warm night, but there's a cool breeze rolling through the Valley. The five of us crowd the footpath and a man with a backpack starts crossing the road when he sees us walking towards him. No one else really notices him. They just continue chatting and laughing, but I watch the man reach the other side of the street and glance back. He's probably terrified of us: five black kids in hoodies.

Only a few blocks over we arrive at another building of units and head through the gates, past the overflowing wheelie bins. There's music playing from one of the units above – Snoop Dogg, if I'm not mistaken. In another unit, a woman and a man yell and their voices vibrate the glass door of the block's entrance.

I follow all the boys inside and then up the stairs. Stevie thumps his fist against the first door at the top of the first flight of stairs. The door opens and there is Jess. She wears a white tank top and tight black jean shorts, which show off her slim thighs and long legs, all the way down to her bare feet. Teresa's standing behind her. She's Aboriginal and short as hell.

''Bout fuckin' time,' Teresa says. The girls step aside and I follow the boys into the living room. An old couch sits against the back wall with a coffee table in front of it. The little TV in the corner of the room plays *Family Guy*. There's another girl who I don't know sitting on the couch. She's white like Jess, but much shorter. She's leaning from her seat over the coffee table, where she is taking her scissors to a bowl and chopping up the weed inside. Beside the bowl is a bong made from a chocolate milk bottle, with a piece of cut hose jammed into its side and scrunch of foil on the end.

'Me first,' Stevie says. Teresa sits with the unnamed white girl on the couch and some of the boys join them. The rest of us sit on the floor, semi-circled around the coffee table. Stevie ignites the lighter and takes a hit from the bong. He coughs a little before he passes it on to Andy. He takes a hit and I snap a photo with my phone. The flash goes off and he stops mid-hit with a flurry of coughs.

'Delete that,' he says. I just laugh at him. He hands off the bong and shuffles his way over to me. 'Jamie, please delete it.'

I'm still pissing myself, but I let him hover his head over my phone to watch me delete the pic.

The bong gets passed around and everyone takes one big hit, except for Stevie, who takes two small ones.

The bong arrives at me. I don't want to be a boring bastard or anything, so I take the smallest puff from the bong anyone has ever taken, then pass the bong to the fulla beside me. Soon enough, music begins. It's some rap song I haven't heard before, playing from someone's phone. It's not very good, either. Oh well. I just lie on my back for a moment and stare at the ceiling.

'Youse got any grog?' Stevie asks the girls.

'Some beer and goon, but we can't drink here too long. Mum'll be home soon,' Teresa says.

'Why don't we go down the youth centre?' Stevie asks. 'Me and my old mates used to go there all the time when we were younger. They leave the side fire exit unlocked in case any kids need to sleep there.'

No one protests. I listen to the sounds of the bottles of grog being bundled into a bag and the zipper being zipped.

I rise to my feet with everyone else. Maybe I can get one good night in before the lads kill me.

28

It's about midnight and the town is dead silent, except for our voices echoing in the sky. The group of us walk from the Valley into town. The youth centre is on the bush side of the main street. It's quiet-looking when we arrive – dark and empty. Stevie twists the knob and the door opens. There is only black when we walk inside.

'Hello?' Stevie calls into the blackness and the echo nearly makes me shit my pants. We head straight for the kitchen. Stevie uses his phone light to find the kitchen's light switch. I go to the fridge, pull out a tray of orange slices, peel back the cling wrap and distribute the pieces to the group.

We all take our drinks and oranges out the back to the basketball courts. It's just bush behind them, so no one from town will see us. We aren't quiet anymore, though.

We sit on the ground and share cigarettes. The girls drink from a half-full goon sack and offer me a sip. I know what I'm in for and as soon as I take a mouthful, I nearly vomit. It's like drinking cold piss with a sprinkle of sugar and a dash of cordial.

Another group of kids show up on the other side of the fence, under the trees and in the shadows of the full moon. They are younger than us, just four dark kids. Maybe aged twelve, or thirteen. Maybe they're those kids who were out the night me, Dally and Lenny stole Mark Cassidy's Mitsubishi. They sort of stare at us for a moment through the fence before they go and find a spot to settle across the basketball courts, away from the moonlight.

The four kids cackle with laughter and my attention draws back to them. I want to go over to them and tell them to get home. I'm sure it's past their bedtime by now. They should be under their blankets instead of doing stupid shit on the streets of Dalton's Bay. It's hard to see them properly in the dark, but I can tell they are over there drinking from their own goon sack. I think I'm sobering up because I finished my beer ages ago and I refuse to drink goon again. The urge to tell them to get home is growing stronger, and I realise something: they remind me of me. I was always wandering the streets at night with Dally and Lenny and the boys, drinking whatever we could get our hands on.

'I'm gonna head home,' Stevie says. A cool breeze is moving through the trees behind the youth centre and there are no clouds in the sky at all. All the stars are on display like Christmas lights in the black.

'Yeah, me too,' Teresa says. 'Mum's probably wondering where I am.'

'I might stay a bit longer,' Jess says, lighting herself a cigarette.

'Me too,' I say.

Stevie leaves with Teresa and two other boys, and I'm left sitting on the ground with Jess and the other white girl, and Andy. Andy is proper wounded, mumbling words that none of us can understand. He gets to his feet and takes himself to the basketball hoop. He pretends to bounce an invisible ball as he approaches the free-throw line, then straightens and flicks his wrists, seeing the invisible ball through the hoop.

Jess takes a mouthful of goon from the cask. She offers it to me. I want to refuse because of the awful taste, but fuck it – I take another mouthful.

Disgusting.

A deathly taste.

Another mouthful.

'You all wanna come back to mine? Got more weed there,' Jess asks, turning to face me as she draws in from her cigarette.

'I'll come over,' I say. Andy nods.

'Sweet,' Jess says. We head back through the youth centre and I lock the door behind me as we go out the front. Time flies by as we make our way back to the Valley.

The grass grows long in Jess's front yard. There are skateboards and scooters and random toys all living on the grass and her parents are on the verandah smoking.

'What do you think you're doing?' Jess's mum calls out, standing at the railing as we step into her yard. I'm surprised her parents are awake.

'Just hanging out, Mum,' Jess replies. She leads us around to the backyard and into the shed.

She's got a couch in there, so I drop my arse onto it. The other white girl takes a big swig from the goon sack. She sits down, rests against the wall and stretches out her legs. Jess pulls a bowl from the shelf and plays some music quietly from her phone. It's Harry Styles. I wasn't really a fan before, but he sounds pretty decent right now.

Jess hands the bowl to me. Inside is a small pipe, resting on a bed of chopped weed, and a lighter. Andy takes the bowl from me and begins to gather some weed into the end of the pipe. He lights it and takes a hit. It's not one minute later when his snores begin. Jess takes the pipe and bowl and gestures them towards me. I shake my head.

'Not a fan of weed?' Jess asks me.

'Nah. Not really,' I say.

The other white girl's eyes are closed. She looks asleep. And Andy is still snoring.

'So,' she says. 'You dating anyone?'

'Nah,' I say. 'No one.'

'Yeah, I'm single too,' Jess says. 'You wanna kiss?'

'Kiss? You want to kiss me?'

'Yeah. Why not?'

I'm too drunk for this. I'm too high for this. I'm too tired for this.

'Nah,' I mumble. 'You had a thing with Dally. I can't.'

Then my eyes close. It's all dark and I can hear myself snoring for a moment.

III

I'm woken by Jess shaking my shoulders. She wakes up the white girl and Andy. He's drooled all over his cheeks.

'You gotta get going,' Jess says. 'My parents will be up soon and it would be better if you're gone.'

Andy and the white girl don't mess around.

'I'll walk back with ya,' Andy says to me.

But I'm too hungover to deal with Andy's motormouth right now. 'Nah, all good. You go ahead.'

They are out of the shed in a minute. I'm groggy as I stand. My head is on fire. I feel the fullness in my stomach, burning and twisting. I stand with Jess and she guides me to the doorway as my mouth fills with saliva. Then, all the vomit in my stomach finds its way to my throat and I blast it at the white wall of her shed. It feels like years have passed by the time I stop vomiting. Some of it splashes off the wall onto Jess's shoulder. The white wall is now painted orange. It drips down towards the floor. All liquid. Not chunky at all.

'What the fuck!' Jess shouts, whacking my shoulder.

I cough as I stumble away, trying to clear my throat. I have to get out of here. I make it outside, to the road, spit over and over and gather all the saliva I can, just so I can spit it onto the bitumen. I need water fast.

The brightness of the morning sky burns my eyes as I walk onto the footpath. Heading into town, it seems like a busy Friday morning, even though it's Saturday. The traffic is racing around and everyone's off to work.

I find a park and there's a little bubbler by the lone park bench. I flick it on and open my mouth. The water flows slowly and I gargle and spit out the vomit left in my mouth, then I drink. I drink so much water that I feel like I need to piss by the time I'm done.

I think over the events of last night. I guess it was fun, but it wasn't the same without Dally and Lenny.

It's one of those classic walks of shame as I come along the dirt road through the bush and back to Aunty Dawn's house. Trey's sitting on the verandah sipping a cup of coffee when I arrive.

'You go out drinking last night?' he asks.

'Yesssss,' I say.

'Is that what you want to do with your life? Just keep partying and messin' around? Getting in trouble and ending up in juvie? You want to end up in Big Boys when you're older? Is that what you want?'

'Fuck off, Trey. You just left me here and pissed off to have your own life. Why do you care so much now?'

I don't close the front door when I walk inside.

'Oi,' Aunty Dawn says, setting herself up on the couch with her headset. 'Cut it out, you boys.'

Trey follows me into my bedroom and shuts the door behind him.

'I didn't just leave you,' he says. 'I had to go out for myself because I was dying here. You know that. It was killing me. I had to leave. If I thought I could look after you then, I would've taken you with me, but I was sixteen, for fuck's sake. You can't keep blaming other people for the shit things in your life, Jamie!'

'Can you just get out?' I say. Trey stands there. He can see my eyes are about to leak. He can see my face is red and hot. 'Get out, please!'

He leaves, slams my door shut. I throw myself on my bed and scream into my pillow. I scream for so long my throat can hardly take it. Then I cry. I cry harder than I've ever cried before, all into my pillow.

29

The hangover really hits in the afternoon. It's so warm outside and the aircon hasn't cooled the house much. I head to the kitchen and pour a glass of water. I down the whole glass in one gulp, so I pour myself another. The house is quieter now. Aunty Dawn's resting back on the couch, headset on her chest, rubbing her eyes.

'You okay, Aunt?'

'Oh, I'm feeling well-fucked, to be honest,' she says. I piss myself laughing. She does too. My ribs are sore by the time I finish, because it might be the first time I've ever heard her swear. 'Don't tell your uncle what I just said. I'll never hear the end of it.'

I rest my elbows on the back of the couch and look down at her.

'Tell me a story, son,' she says. 'One I haven't heard before.'

I think of telling her about juvie, about the time I participated in a revolt and climbed onto the roof. I think of telling her about Alex, and how he was the worst of the screws. I think about telling her about the car chase and about how thrilling and scary it was at the same time.

'One of the workers at Kinston…' I begin. 'Her name was Shae. She was really nice, you know. She wasn't like the screws. She taught me about poems and before I left, she gave me a book of poetry. I never really liked any of that before, but she was a really good teacher. I mean, she wasn't a *teacher*, but she taught me about why people write poems. She taught me that I could say things with them, important things, things I felt. So anyway, we decided to write a poem each and read them to each other. And I was stressin'. Like, what would I write a poem about? I didn't think I knew how to say the things I really felt, you know. I decided to write a poem about you. I didn't think it was very good, but Shae said she liked it. She called me clever.'

'That's really nice, son. Will you read it to me? The poem?'

'Well, I dunno. It's a bit embarrassing,' I say. I sip the rest of my water from the glass. 'You probably won't like it.'

'I will. I know I will,' Aunty Dawn says. I sit at her feet and watch the afternoon news. It's not five minutes until she's snoring. Her eyes are closed and she looks real peaceful.

Aunty Dawn's still asleep on the couch when Trey and Uncle Bobby get home. Trey's avoiding looking at me. Uncle Bobby pulls out his wallet and takes out two fifty-dollar notes, which he hands to Trey.

'Go grab some groceries, hey?' Uncle Bobby says. 'We need some food in this house. Take Jamie with ya.'

I follow Trey out to his car. His dashboard says it's thirty-eight degrees Celsius, and I'm definitely feeling it, 'cause there are two dark patches under my armpits.

'I'm sorry I yelled at you earlier,' Trey says. 'I just... I need you to know you can be doing better things with your life. You need to start making better decisions.'

'Like what?' I ask.

'Like, I dunno, saying no when that Stevie idiot tries to get all you kids to go drink with him. He's going nowhere in life.'

'That's what Aunty Dawn always says about him.' I chuckle. 'But we're not *kids*.'

'You're sixteen. You're a kid.'

'Sixteen's not a *kid*, Trey. You were doing the same kind of shit when you were sixteen. Worse, probably.'

'Yeah, but I was really struggling,' Trey says. 'I've made better decisions since then. If you're gonna take after me in any way, take after that.'

He's really going overboard with this big-brother thing, but it is nice to have him around again.

Trey grabs a trolley before we head into the shopping centre. We go into Coles and it's the usual stuff we fill the trolley with: two packets of Weet-Bix, a jar of instant coffee and a box of teabags, a packet of Tim Tams and one of Scotch fingers, mince, lamb chops, frozen vegetables, five bucks' worth of devon and a bunch of bananas.

'Wanna cook with me tonight?' Trey asks as he picks up a packet of chicken breasts. 'We'll make a chicken curry for Aunty Dawn and Uncle Bobby. You can help, build your cooking skills.'

'Yeah.'

'I'm leaving next Friday,' Trey says. 'My dog's missing me, apparently. Her name is Valerie. Jacob says she's been waiting at the door recently, thinking I'll be coming through at any moment.'

'Next Friday?'

'Yeah, so cook dinner with me tonight.'

We stroll into the aisle with all the deodorants and I see Travis. He's holding a can of Brut, reading the back.

'I'll go say hey to Travis,' I say.

'Travis?' Trey asks, spotting him.

'Jamie,' Travis says as I approach. He holds out his hand and I shake it. 'How's it goin', brother?'

'All good,' I say. He looks Trey up and down and then looks into his eyes.

'Trey Langton,' he says, like he can't believe he's seeing Trey. 'I hardly recognised ya.'

'Yeah, I've come a long way since high school, I guess,' Trey says, shaking Travis's hand. 'Looks like you've come a long way, too. Youth worker, hey?'

'Yeah,' Travis replies, then he turns to me. 'Funny I run into you, Jamie. I'm doing another youth camp in a few weeks. It would be great if you could come along. You'd get out of school again.'

'I dunno,' I say. 'Maybe.'

'Cool,' Travis says. 'Andy's coming, I think. So, you'll have a mate there. Plus you'll get to make some new friends. We're heading south this time. I'll count you in?'

I sigh. 'Yeah, maybe. I'll get back to ya.'

Travis shakes my hand again and tries to walk past us, but Trey holds out his arm and stops him.

'Don't you think I deserve an apology?' Trey says.

Travis studies Trey's arm. 'What?' Travis asks, a half-smile on his face.

'Come on,' Trey says, and I have no fucking idea what's going on. 'You remember how you were to me when we were in school. There's no way you've forgotten that.'

Travis swallows hard, looking down.

'You know how it was back then. We were dumb kids,' Travis says. Trey doesn't move. He could be a statue. 'I'm sorry I was an arsehole. You didn't deserve the shit we said to you.'

Trey lowers his arm and starts walking down the aisle. Travis is quick to walk away too, and I'm left standing there with the trolley.

We pay for the food and I wheel the trolley back to the car.

'What was that about?' I ask. 'You gonna say anything? You haven't said a word since...whatever that was.'

'Just put the stuff in the back,' Trey says, getting into the car. I load the groceries and climb into the passenger's seat. Trey lets out a deep breath as we drive back through town.

'Well?' I ask.

'He was a bully,' Trey says, biting his bottom lip. 'Him and his mates used to call me names. *Fag. Poof. Pillow-biter.* I didn't even really know what I was then. It's funny to see he's a youth worker now. He's helping kids who don't know who they are yet, or what their place in the world is, just like me when I was a teenager. Felt like a good time to get that apology he owed me.'

I'm imagining Travis pushing my brother to the dirt and calling him a *poof*. A part of me wants to tell him to shove his camp up his arse. But Trey isn't the same as he was when he was my age. I don't think Travis is that same person either.

'I guess people can change, though, right?' I ask.

'Yeah. People can change.'

We head over the hill, out of the main street and back to Aunty Dawn's place. We load the groceries inside and Trey starts unpacking. I head to my room and before I can plug my phone into my charger, a message arrives on my screen from Mark Cassidy.

You ready to pay me back for what you and your mates did? You're dead boy…

My heart begins to race. I stick my fingers into the top of my shirt to relieve the tightness around my neck.

'Shit,' I whisper to myself. I sit on my bed. I rub my temples with my index fingers. I've got a headache coming.

My phone vibrates on my bedside table. *Maybe another death threat.* I check my phone. It's a message from Dally to our group.

I'm out fuckers. Got back to DB today. Coming over to get pissed Jamie?

240

30

I head out of my room and pass the kitchen where Trey is chopping up the chicken breast.

'I'm gonna go see Dally. He got out of lock-up today,' I say.

'But we're cooking dinner together, aren't we?'

'I want to see Dally.'

Trey sighs. 'You'll be back for dinner, yeah?'

'I'll try to be,' I say.

I head out the door and walk fast to Dally's place. It's pretty warm and the sun hasn't set yet.

Dally's garage door is open and he's sitting inside with his dad having a beer. Dally stands and rushes to me, then greets me with a hug. He seems taller somehow. He's put on weight since I last saw him and he's let his facial hair grow a bit – it's more than just ten strands of hair now.

'We made it,' he says.

'Good to see ya.'

'You want a beer? Or a bourbon?' he asks, heading to the bar fridge.

'Actually, I don't really feel like drinking. My brother's down for a bit and I'm helping him cook dinner tonight.'

'What? Don't be silly. You can still have a drink,' Dally says. He can see I'm hesitant. 'Come on, we haven't seen each other in months. Just have a couple, then you can piss off home and cook.'

I sigh. 'Fine. I'll take a beer.'

'I'll get out of your hair,' Dally's dad says as he heads inside. 'Cricket's on if youse wanna come in and watch.'

I take a seat on the couch.

'How was it for you?' Dally asks, joining me. 'They sent me to Grenville. I swear, bruh, it was ninety per cent Kooris. It was as small as a couple of houses squashed together.'

'Yeah? They put me in Kinston. Fair few Kooris in there too. Lots of different kids, though. It was a pretty big place.'

'I feel like we've been *initiated* now,' Dally says. 'Like Travis was saying at camp last year. Like a rite of passage. We're part of the crew now, or something.'

'I don't think Travis was talking about going to jail when he was talking about growing up,' I say.

'Don't ya reckon?'

Dally plays some music quietly from his bluetooth speaker – ScHoolboy Q. He rests back on the couch and sips his beer.

'It was pretty shit being locked up, though, right?' I ask.

'Shit? Nah, it was okay. Just, like, kickin' back with the mob. We did whatever we wanted in Grenville, really. I was the oldest one there, I reckon. Most of the boys in there been in and out a few times.'

I finish my beer and find myself drinking another. Before I know it, it's sunset and eight o'clock. Three of the boys come over and Dally brings his Xbox and TV to the garage so we can play Halo.

By nine p.m., Dally's strutting around his garage in his tank top, flexing the muscles he was working on in lock-up. I can't help but think something's changed in Dally. He's more confident now, and he was already the most confident of all of us.

'We should head into town for a walk,' Dally says. 'Maybe we'll run into Mark and Porter and teach 'em a lesson. Check this.'

Dally shows me his phone. It's a thread of messages from Mark Cassidy, sent over the last few months, and the most recent message, Dally has replied to.

Let me know when you get back to Daltons Bay so I can get my knife sharpened.

Catch me if you can, Marky boy.

'They've been threatening me too, you know? They want to get back at us for what we did.'

'Yeah, their silly threats were blowing up my phone when I finally turned it on. Let 'em try,' Dally says. 'Fuck 'em. They won't dare touch us. Surely his daddy's bought him another car. Let's take his new car for a spin, but we'll set it on fire this time.'

'No way in hell.' I giggle.

The boys head home around ten o'clock and after only having one drink each. Dally says he's going to Stevie's.

'Coming with me?' Dally asks me.

'Nah, I'm tired.'

'Come on. Don't be a pussy.'

'I'm not being a pussy,' I say, standing. 'I'm gonna head home.'

'Fine. Well, it was good to see ya,' Dally says, shaking my hand.

'You too.'

'Meet me at the youth centre after school on Friday?' Dally asks. 'We'll kick back.'

'Yeah, all right.'

I make yet another walk of shame back through the Valley, past the streetlight and into the bush to Aunty Dawn's.

The house is dark when I get back. The front door is unlocked like always, so I take off my shoes and sneak across the wooden floor. The light is on under the door of the spare room. I open my creaky bedroom door, slip inside and get into bed.

III

My head feels like it's been filled with rocks when I wake up at six a.m. It's Sunday morning and I head to the bathroom for a vomit. I spray it into the toilet and it's all liquid.

I head to the kitchen and make myself a bowl of Weet-Bix. Uncle Bobby comes out dressed in his Steve Irwin gear for work at the national park.

'Aunt's not feeling too well,' he says, turning the kettle on. 'Probably the heat. Reckon I might call in sick to look after her.'

I turn to see Trey coming out of the spare room with his duffel bag packed.

'Morning,' Uncle Bobby says to Trey.

'Morning, Unk,' Trey says. 'I'm gonna head back home today. I can't take any more time off work.'

'Oh. All right,' Uncle Bobby says.

Trey doesn't even look at me as he heads outside. I watch him through the windows as he packs the bag into the boot of his car. He comes back in and makes a bowl of Weet-Bix.

'I thought you were heading back on Friday,' I say.

'I changed my mind.'

Uncle Bobby makes his coffee and heads to his bedroom, then it's just me and Trey at the table.

'I wanted to cook dinner with you last night,' he says. 'I thought we could do that together. You know? I thought it would be nice. I could have taught you how to make a good curry. You said you'd try to be back, but you weren't.'

'I'm sorry.'

Trey sighs. 'It's time to pull your head in,' he says. 'I mean it. You're better than what you're doing. You're better than your little mates. You're smart. I know you are. Pull your head in. Tell me you will.'

'What you goin' on about?' I ask. I can't help it. I know he is trying to be fully serious right now, but for some reason I feel like laughing.

'Jamie,' he says with a sigh. 'Just…Just call me once in a while, yeah? No more long breaks of no talking. Keep me updated. I want to know how you're going.'

I nod. 'I'll call you on the weekend.'

'Promise?' he asks.

'Promise. I will.'

I follow Trey outside and stop on the verandah. Trey starts his car and reverses out of his spot. He stops at the foot of the driveway, looks to me through the window. Trey gives a little wave, which I return, then he drives away. My phone buzzes. When I check the screen, there's a message from Mark Cassidy:

I heard your stupid mate is out of juvie. Better watch your backs.

31

The lads are all I've thought about all week. I can feel them coming for me. It's like there's a clock on my chest and the time is slowly ticking down on me. It's ticking down on Dally, too.

It's Friday afternoon and the worry in my stomach is strong as I wait outside the English room for class to begin.

And I still feel so bad for the way Trey left. I'm such a shit brother. I'm not worth sticking around for, but I wish he'd stayed. I wish I'd cooked the chicken curry with him.

Mr Barrett arrives and opens the classroom door for us. He's finally back. Before class starts, he gestures with his finger for me to come up to his desk.

'Jamie,' he says as I take a seat. 'How are you finding the classes since you've come back?'

'They're all right,' I say. 'I'm still catching up.'

'If you could describe last year in one word, what word would you choose?' he asks. There's a slight smile on his face, like he's running some kind of secret test on me.

'I don't think it would be appropriate for me to use that word in front of a teacher,' I say.

Mr Barrett chuckles and nods. 'I came across the poem you wrote – the one in your English book. You might have noticed that I marked it,' he says. 'Obviously there are no grades to be won there, but I thought it was quite exceptional. I was wondering if you could do something for me.'

'What's that?'

'I want you to write another poem. Free verse. I want you to reflect on your time in juvenile detention. Think about how it affected you, how you dreamed, how your heart felt.'

'How my *heart* felt?'

'I know it sounds silly,' he says, with a warm smile on his face now. '*Expression*. Take all those dark places you've been to and turn them into poetry, at least just for this one free-verse poem. It's not real homework, I must stress. I thought it might be a good task for you personally. Maybe you'll find you really enjoy writing poetry. And of course, I would really enjoy reading it.'

'Hmm.'

'Don't overthink it.'

I head to my desk.

'Okay, class. Today will be a quiet reading lesson. So, if you've got a book to read, great! If not, go grab one from the back shelf. There will be no using phones – this is time for reading. Get those brain muscles of yours warm.'

I grab *The Absolutely True Diary of a Part-time Indian* from the shelf and bring it back to my desk. I finish reading the second half and close it on my desk. There's still

248

twenty-five minutes left of class and I'm feeling inspired. The book was the first time I've read an Indigenous story. It was funny, sad and beautiful all at once. I want to write like that.

I open my exercise book to a blank page. Mr Barrett wants me to write a poem. I try to remember the poetry I've read, and what Shae told me: *You've got a voice inside you, Jamie... It's really powerful the way she basically blasts him with the full force of her heart.*

I jot down the title at the top of the page: 'The Dark Place'.

When I look at that title, I'm surprised because instead of thinking about my time in juvie, thoughts of Mum and Dad come rushing in. Well, not thoughts of *them*, but thoughts of the fuzziness, the scramble in my mind when I try to think about them. I think about how every moment in my life has led me to the next. I wouldn't have gone to juvie if some white person sitting in an office hadn't decided one day that Mum and Dad weren't good enough parents for me and Trey. I don't think I would have stolen that car with Dally and Lenny if I was still living with Mum and Dad. My life would have been more normal and I wouldn't be the boy in foster care. My memories wouldn't be so fuzzy. If I were looking at my life as photos in an album, my time in juvie would be a black square. I'd choose for my time there to be black, if it meant I could have another picture, clear as day, of me with my mum and dad when I was little.

I shift in my seat as an idea comes to me – a series of words. Beneath the title, I quickly jot down my free-verse poem. It's kind of like that feeling I had when I was writing the poem for Shae, and the one about Shae – the feeling when the perfect words all come to me at once – but it's much stronger than before.

32

After school, I head to the youth centre in town. Dally's inside, resting back on a beanbag under the path of the airconditioner, texting on his phone. He's got a fresh black eye.

'What happened?' I ask.

'Nothin'. Just had a bit of a scuffle with Dad,' Dally says. I know Dally well enough to know he doesn't want me to pry.

'They won't let me continue my apprenticeship,' Dally says. 'Shit's fucked.'

'Because of juvie?'

'Yeah,' Dally says. He hangs his head.

'Don't worry, you can just go somewhere else.'

'Dad rang the plumbers over north as well. They won't take me. Reckon they already got an apprentice.'

I wish I had the perfect words to say, but I don't. Sausages are sizzling on the barbecue out the back. The smell finds its way inside the youth centre and gets my mouth watering.

'The lads passed me when I was just getting here,' Dally says. 'They slowed right down and stopped in the middle of the road, gave me a good death stare. I stuck my finger up at 'em and told 'em to fuck off.'

'Nice,' I say. 'I'm surprised they haven't killed us already.'

'I'd like to see 'em try. I got more important things to worry about, like where the hell I'm gonna get a job. Oh, Stevie's having a party tomorrow night. He said we could come, so I told him me and you would go. You down?'

'Yeah, maybe.'

I sit down and let the cool air wash over me.

'So what are you gonna do? Thinking of coming back to school?' I ask.

'Nah, fuck that. I'd have to repeat and then I'd be a *real* failure. I applied for a job at Target and did one of them online applications for the KFC on the highway. Only problem is, I'm banned from getting my licence for four years,' Dally says. 'Dad's not too happy with me about losing the apprenticeship, and he's right. I fucked up.'

Travis comes inside to tell us the sausages are ready. It's like a million degrees when I get outside. A couple of the Koori boys I recognise from camp are shooting hoops on the court. Andy and one of the boys are passing the footy to each other in the shade by the fence. Me and Dally get our sausages and head up the back to eat.

It's nice in the shade. Cool breeze, warm pavement. It makes me think of old times.

'Hey,' I say to Dally. 'Remember when we were around ten or eleven years old, and me, you and Lenny packed our swimmers and got on the bus?'

Dally chuckles, nearly choking on his sausage sandwich.

'When we caught the bus all the way to the beach without telling anyone?'

'Yeah.' I smile. 'We spent the day swimming and exploring the rockpools. We found that crab and you and Lenny were too scared to pick it up, but I remembered my mum had taught me to pick them up by the arse.'

'I wanted to kill you.' Dally laughs, looking to the sky, remembering. 'You picked up the crab and chased me and Lenny down the beach with it.'

I laugh until my stomach hurts because I remember the looks on their faces as they ran while I chased them with a crab, pincers out front.

'Why the hell didn't we tell anyone where we were going? Aunty Dawn was so angry when we got back, but Uncle Bobby was mostly laughing.'

'I dunno. We were just doing things, we weren't really thinking. Lenny got off the easiest, hey,' Dally says.

'Yeah. His parents told him not to hang with us anymore, but he was back soon enough.'

It was a hot day like today when we'd snuck off to the beach. Dally checks the weather app on his phone. It's not meant to cool down until after eight o'clock and there's a fifty per cent chance of rain. We decide to chill inside the youth centre.

As it starts to get dark outside, everyone at the youth centre begins to leave. Travis puts a movie on the telly for those of us who are still there: *Chicken Run*. I haven't seen this movie in years and it's still hilarious, even though I'm older now. Dally snoozes off when we get to the part where the chickens find out Rocky is a stunt performer.

The rain begins to fall lightly outside as the movie finishes. It's just after nine-thirty and Travis and one of the other youth workers starts cleaning up.

'Time to head home, boys,' Travis says. I nudge Dally and he jolts like I've woken him from a terrible nightmare. He gasps and presses his hand on his chest and I can't help but giggle.

'How long was I out for?' Dally asks.

'I dunno. An hour, maybe,' I say. 'Come on, they're closing up.'

It's still warm outside, but the rain is really cooling.

'Can your dad pick us up?' I ask. 'Feels like it's gonna piss down.'

'Nah he's drinkin'. It's just a sprinkle, we'll be right. I'm craving a Coke,' Dally says, checking the time on his phone. 'Come on, the shopping centre shuts in fifteen.'

He starts running along the footpath, into the rain. I follow him onto the main street. I've got sweat all over me, but the rain's washing it away.

We run to the big car park behind the shopping centre. There are a few cars still there – one of them is a white Holden Trax. It looks like Mark's car, but it could belong to anyone.

We get to the entrance and head inside. I'm panting like a dog as the airconditioning blasts us. A security guard's standing by the service desk on his phone, but looks up as our wet shoes flap on the floor.

'Slow down, no running,' he says.

'Sorry,' me and Dally say together. The security guard takes his eyes back to his phone. We slow to a walk and I follow Dally to the vending machine.

He starts loading his coins into the slot. I notice Porter Davis walking out of Woolies. He's with one of the lads, carrying a box of flavoured icy poles. They're talking about something, but they stop when they see us, then they stare as they walk past.

Dally's can of Coke rumbles to the bottom of the vending machine and scares me. He opens the can and takes a sip. I nod my head in Porter's direction. Dally turns to see them. The lads turn their backs on us and continue out of the shopping centre.

'Come on, we'll head out the front,' Dally says.

We start for the front of the shopping centre, which exits to the main street, but I can see the security doors are already down.

'You'll have to go out the back door,' the security guard calls.

'Fuck me,' Dally says. He turns to me. 'You got me, right?'

'Yeah,' I say. 'I got you.'

We walk slowly to the doorway at the back of the shopping centre. My heart is racing at a thousand miles a minute. I think I can hear Dally's heart beating too.

The automatic doors slide open and we step outside. An engine is rumbling in the car park – the white Holden Trax. It's dark and still raining, but under the shine of the car park's lights, I can see Mark Cassidy in the driver's seat and the car filled with lads.

The engine revs, then the headlights come on. They're about fifty metres away and the only way out is the car park exit to our left.

'Go!' Dally shouts. We start sprinting. The bottoms of my shoes are slippery in the wet, but I run as fast as I can.

The tyres spin on the Holden Trax and the beams of the headlights stream across the air, catching the raindrops ahead of me. We're close to the exit, so close, but not fast enough – the Holden Trax speeds in front of us. The tyres screech as the car zooms across the exit. It comes to a halt. Mark Cassidy has this evil look of joy on his face, same as the look Dally had in his eyes the night we stole his car. Mark revs his engine, daring us to run again.

33

Me and Dally race across the car park, running for the steel fences surrounding the shops beside the shopping centre. My foot lands in a puddle and splashes all through my socks. Dally pulls up quick ahead of me when the Holden Trax comes swerving across the empty parking spaces in front of us. The lads come to a halt again, howling with laughter like maniacs.

Dally drops his can of Coke and starts running towards the exit. Mark spins his tyres and drifts across Dally's path again. Dally backs up to me as the Holden Trax slowly drives towards him.

The high beams come on and Mark blasts the horn before braking. The five of them get out of the car.

'Youse ain't goin' nowhere,' Mark says, as they form a wall, moving in on us. They're all dressed in white linen shirts and jeans. Mark's jeans are black and his shirt is short-sleeved.

'Youse are so dead.' Porter giggles.

'Fuck off, Porter,' Dally says.

'No, *you* fuck off, junkie,' Mark shouts. 'You've had this coming for a long time. You'll never so much as look at a car of mine again. You see me coming down the street, you walk the other way. You see me driving by, you drop to the ground so I don't have to look at your ugly face.'

Mark unbuttons his shirt and takes it off. He's wearing a white singlet underneath. I can't help but be distracted by my wet socks and shoes squeaking with every step backwards I take. We reach the brick wall and there's no further we can go. We're trapped.

'My family owns this town,' Mark says. 'You fuckers are just cockroaches on the floor. No one gives a fuck about you.'

'We're not gonna fight you,' Dally says, and it surprises me. His voice is shaky and he's puffing. 'We don't *want* to fight.'

'Oh, we're fighting, all right. Me and you,' Mark says, pointing to Dally. 'You're the retard who crashed my car. You're the one who's gonna pay.'

'I'm sorry, okay?' Dally says, his back against the wall. 'We shouldn't've taken your car. All right? I'm sorry. *We're* sorry.'

Mark and the others burst into laughter like it's overcoming them.

'Dally,' I say, trying to get him to stop sounding so scared. I once thought Dally was the toughest boy I'd ever met.

'You're not so brave without your little crew around ya,' Mark says. 'You're making me sad, boy.'

'Who you callin' *boy*?' I say, stepping in front of Dally. I can smell Mark's bad breath from here.

'What you gonna do? If *he's* too scared to fight me, then what good are *you*?' Mark says, and it's hard to tell if it's the rain or his saliva hitting my face. 'You blackfellas never learn.'

'I'll fight you,' I say. I'm surprised those are the words that come out of my mouth. It's like a rising heat inside me, that tells me it's time to take a stand – to stand up to not just Mark, but Alex and Sergeant Hudson too. 'I'll fight you.'

'Jamie, don't,' Dally says, grabbing me by the shoulder.

'Step back, Dal,' I say. The words of my father rush into my mind from that time we went camping and fishing:

It's a moment that makes a man. A decision.

The other lads cheer and woof like dogs as Mark stretches his arms and cracks his neck. He's a big boy; he's got muscles. He's got strong arms and big fists. He's puffing out his chest. He's smiling. He can't get enough of this situation.

I'm still in my school uniform. I'm expecting Sergeant Hudson and Constable Minelli to rock up with some popcorn at any moment.

'You sure you wanna do this?' Mark asks, looking me up and down.

'Yep. This fight is it. It all ends here. All of it. Just you and me,' I say.

Mark nods a few times. 'Something will be *ending*, that's for sure.'

He takes a swing at me and I dodge it. Dally's still just standing there looking like a scared puppy desperate to seek shelter from the rain.

Mark comes for me again, launches his fist at my face, but I duck. I land a punch to his stomach and he steps away.

'There you go,' he says, smiling.

He moves towards me again. I take a swing. My fist collects the side of his jaw and he shoves me back.

'That the best you got, boy?' he jests. The rain starts falling heavier. The drops land in my eyes and it's hard to see.

A bang on my chest forces me to one knee. I hear the footy boys laughing as all the air escapes my lungs.

'Get up, boy. Come on,' Mark says. I take a breath, try to get the air back into my lungs. Three more deep breaths, then I'm on my feet.

A bang on my mouth lands me on my arse. Rain pours down on me. My mouth feels numb. There's blood on my tongue. My vision is blurred and I'm dizzy.

'Up ya get,' Mark says. The others are howling with laughter, calling me names.

I wipe the rain from my eyes, feel my lips with my fingers. When I look at my fingertips, they are covered in red, but the rain washes the blood away.

'Get up, Jamie,' Dally says. He's standing there above me, caught in the high-beams, hair all wet and splayed across his forehead.

I force my palms to the cement, push myself to my feet. I straighten my back and look Mark in the eye. He launches his fist at my face. I try to dodge, but I'm too slow and he hits my jaw. I fall again. Dally tries to catch me, but I slip through his hands and to the wet cement.

'Now, you gonna stay down like a good little boy?' Mark asks. Porter's laughing and so are the others. I rise from the wet and plant my feet. As I spring up, I aim my fist at Mark's stomach. My punch doesn't affect him at all.

A blow to my stomach folds me forward. Mark gets me in a headlock, then his knee strikes my stomach over and over. All the air leaves my body again and I close my eyes. It feels like my ribs are breaking, like blood is rushing around inside me. The headlock releases and Mark shoves me back. My head thumps onto the cement.

'Jamie,' Dally says. 'It's all right. Stay down.'

'Yeah, stay down, pussy.' Mark cackles.

I hate him. I hate him so much. And as the rain falls on my face, I hear the voice of my father again.

It's a moment that makes a man. A decision.

I make my decision: I get up.

'That the best *you* got, *boy*?' I say. A smile comes to my face and I don't know why. Mark's grin is gone and his expression has changed to a frown. His white face has turned red. He's got a fire in his eyes – a rage. It's probably the rage he felt when he heard three blackfullas stole his car and took it for a joyride. It's the rage I want to see, to feel.

Mark comes for me again, fists out front.

I feel the power surge from the bottom of my foot to the top of my shoulder, like electricity. I pull my fist back like a slingshot and launch it. His nose pops beneath my knuckles and his arms wave. He falls to the ground, face-first, splashing water onto my knees. He's making some noise, kind of like a moan.

The lads are all quiet now. Porter's the first to go to Mark, keeping his eyes on me, then the rest of them follow him. They roll Mark onto his side and try to wake him up. His eyes open and he looks up to them. The anger has always been there for me when no one else was, but it's not here now. I'm looking down at Mark and I don't see the tough boy I was so scared of, I don't feel the rage I want to feel. There's only pity.

'What happened?' Mark mumbles to his mates. 'Did I win?'

'Come on,' I say to Dally. 'Let's get outta here.'

The lads don't follow us as we walk out of the car park and down the main street of Dalton's Bay. We head up the hill towards the Valley and my lip is stinging.

'Jamie, you are a bad motherfucker,' Dally says. 'You iced that bastard. You destroyed him. I didn't know you had it in ya.'

'Neither did I,' I say.

The rain eases off as we come into the Valley. We arrive at Dally's driveway and he's still going on about how I beat Mark Cassidy – how I made a fool of him.

'Let's get pissed now, bruh,' Dally says. 'You deserve it.'

Dally rolls up his garage door and I follow him inside. I take a seat on the couch and Dally brings me a beer. I'm replaying the fight over and over in my head. I'm re-creating the pop I felt when my fist landed on Mark's nose. My heart is racing and even though I'm soaking wet, I'm as hot as a stream of lava.

'Ain't no one gonna mess with you now,' Dally says. 'Wait 'til all the boys hear about this. You'll be the most feared blackfulla in Dalton's Bay.'

'*Most feared?*' I ask as I twist the lid off my beer.

'Yeah,' Dally says, brimming with excitement. '*We* own this town, bruh. *You* own it.'

He takes down half of his beer with one gulp.

'I don't want to *own* it,' I say, looking at my beer. The knuckles on my right hand are red and beginning to swell. My hand is stinging, so I hold the cold beer bottle against the back of it. My top lip is beginning to swell too, and I can feel it fattening as I run my tongue over it.

'What you mean?' Dally asks, taking another sip.

'I'm going home.' I stand from the couch and walk to Dally, hand him the undrunk beer.

'What are you on about?' Dally asks.

'I'm going home,' I say.

'You sure you don't wanna charge? After that fight?' Dally asks, screwing his face up at me.

'Nah,' I say. It falls quiet between us, thick as the humidity in the air. The rain's stopped falling, so there's not even that to distract us.

'You're serious?' he asks. 'Are you right?'

'Yeah. I'm just going home,' I say.

Dally nods and takes another sip of his beer.

'Well, you still coming to Stevie's tomorrow?'

'I dunno. Maybe,' I say.

'Okay, cool.'

I'm not going to Stevie's. I'm not going to drink with Dally tomorrow night. I didn't know it before, but I don't want to be like Stevie. I don't want to be like Dally. Like the words of my free-verse poem, it all comes rushing to me. *A moment. A decision.* I walk out of the garage, down the driveway. I don't feel angry anymore. I thought I would, but I just feel tired.

'See ya tomorrow,' Dally calls from his garage door. I can feel him watching me, waiting for me to stop, turn back to him and say I'll see him tomorrow too, but I won't. I won't turn back.

I pass the streetlight and head into the bush, follow Aunty Dawn's driveway through the darkness to her house. I pull my phone from my pocket and search for Trey in my contacts. The phone rings a few times before he answers.

Trey clears his throat. 'Jamie? Everything okay?'

'Yeah,' I say, approaching Aunty Dawn's house. I can see Aunty Dawn and Uncle Bobby through the window. They're sitting on the couch, their bodies lit by the telly.

'What's up?' Trey asks.

'Can I come to your place?' I ask. 'You said I could come.'

'To live with me?'

'I don't know. Maybe. Can I come or not?' I ask. The tears have found their way to my eyes and my throat is feeling scratchy. 'I need to get out of this place.'

'Why? What's happened?'

'Trey, dickhead. I'm asking you a question.'

'Jamie,' Trey says. His voice sounds strong suddenly. 'Did something bad happen? Are you in trouble again?'

'No, I just…I can't…'

A knot in my throat. A burning in my eyes. My face is hot and the tears break from my eyes and roll down my cheeks.

'I'm just over it,' I say. 'I'm over it.'

'You're *over it*?' Trey asks.

'It's not who I am. It's not me. It's not who I wanna be.'

'What are you talking about, Jamie?'

'Dally,' I say. 'I can't keep following him. The lads, the boys, the Valley…I'm sick of it all. I want out.'

'Okay,' Trey says.

I sniffle, try to wipe my eyes.

'Jamie?' Trey asks.

'Yeah?'

'We'll figure it out. But you can't just up and leave, okay? I'd love to have you live with me, but there's stuff we need to sort out first.'

A minute passes by where we don't say anything, just breathe together through the phone.

'Trey,' I say.

'Yeah?'

'I'm ready to see Mum and Dad again.'

'You are?'

I wipe away the tears and clear my throat.

'Yeah. I think I am,' I say.

After I hang up, I wait until Aunty Dawn and Uncle Bobby leave the lounge room and the lights turn off before

I go inside. I close the door quietly behind me and tiptoe into my room. I kick off my shoes, take off my clothes and get in bed. It somehow feels like everything will be different when I wake up in the morning. I guess it will be different, because for the first time in a long time, I'm falling asleep knowing that soon I'll be seeing my mum and dad.

The offices had white walls at Family Services. There were photos of happy white kids on them – hugging adults, smiling, playing with toys. I was sitting on the floor and the carpet was making the backs of my legs itchy. Trey was standing in the corner of the room with his arms folded, beside the tall white woman in the black blouse and business pants. She had a square face, glasses and grey hair, but she didn't look very old.

The door opened and Mum and Dad were on the other side. Mum's eyes were red and her hair was messy, but she smiled the biggest smile when she walked in. I rushed to her and we hugged. Trey came over and hugged Mum too.

'My babies,' she said.

'I missed you, Mum,' I said.

'I missed you too, baby,' she said. She glanced at the tall woman and took me to the floor, where we sat down with Trey and Dad.

'Has Aunty been feeding youse right?' Dad asked.

'Yeuh. We had spaghetti and meatballs last night,' Trey said.

'How's school going?' Mum asked. She turned to Trey. 'Trey, how's school?'

'It's fine,' Trey said.

'Are we going with you and Dad?' I asked. 'I want to go home.'

'Not right now, baby,' Mum said. She glanced at the tall woman again. 'First, me and Dad have to get a new house.

When we do, we'll make you and Trey a room and then you can both come home.'

The tall woman cleared her throat behind us. 'Kate, we talked about appropriate responses, remember?'

Mum nodded. 'Don't worry, baby,' she whispered to me. 'We just need you and your brother to stay with Aunty Dawn for a bit longer, then we'll bring you home.'

'You promise?'

'Be mindful of your responses,' the tall woman interrupted, and Mum looked at her.

'Let's talk about it next time,' Mum said to me. She grabbed the plastic bag Dad was carrying. She pulled out an Xbox game and handed it to me. It was Splinter Cell. 'You like that one, don't you?'

'Yeah, it's all right,' I said. 'Will me and Trey have to share a bunk bed again when we come home?'

'No,' Dad said.

'We'll get you your own beds next time,' Mum said. 'And you'll have your own room, and Trey will have his own room too.'

The tall woman came over to us. She said something, but I couldn't hear because Mum was hugging me.

'I love you both very, very much,' she said. She hugged me so tight and warm that I thought I might fall asleep in her arms.

34

Three weeks have passed since I beat Mark Cassidy in a fight, and it's also been three weeks since I last talked to Dally. I made a decision when I left Kinston, that I wouldn't end up in that place again. I made a decision when I stood up to Mark Cassidy, that I would end the war with them. My decision is to do better.

I'm waiting outside English class, reading the last message Dally sent me from three days ago:

I got a job doin plumbing. Call me Kenny from now on lol.

I haven't replied. I don't think I will. I'm glad he's doing something, but I need to keep in my own lane for a bit. Besides, tomorrow morning I'm catching the bus to Sydney, then me and Trey are going to The Entrance to see Mum and Dad.

Word got around school pretty fast that I knocked Mark Cassidy out, and the past three weeks have been weird, because I feel like everyone's looking at me when I walk around school. I've noticed girls staring at me, and I'm not really used to that. News of my victory has sort of fizzled out now, but I still feel the looks.

Mr Barrett stops me before I walk into English class.

'I absolutely loved your poem, Jamie. "The Dark Place". A fabulous title. I'd love it if you could read it to the class today. What do you think?'

I feel my palms and my neck become sweaty suddenly.

'Oh, nah, I can't do that. Sorry.'

'Would you mind if *I* read it to the class?' he asks.

I feel my heart pounding. They'll all hate it. They'll all make fun of me. They'll call me *poetry-boy*, which I guess is at least better than *juvie-boy*.

'Okay,' I say. I head inside and take a seat at my desk.

Mr Barrett stands at the front of the class.

'Everyone, quieten down. I have something to read to you,' he says. Silence fills the room. Mr Barrett clears his throat.

'It's all fun at the start

Until it's white walls and rules.

In the dark place, schedule owns you.

You are theirs to play with.

You are alone but surrounded.

Surrounded by black faces.

Black faces of black kids.

Black children.

The white men rule in the dark place.

The black children abide.

They cry out for the old people

To save us from ourselves.

Dangers to society.

Troubled youth, of no good.
We are there in the dark place
And in and out we come.
In and out we come.
Black children, ruled by white men.
A cycle.
A circle.
We're stuck in the stream.
But those who dare to,
Reach out their arms.
Those who dare to,
Find a branch.
Those who dare to,
Grab that branch and pull.
One arm after the other.
One arm after the other.'

It's over. My heart rate slows. I wipe my sweaty palms on my lap and take a deep breath.

'That wonderful poem,' Mr Barrett says, 'was written by none other than our own James Langton.'

I wait for the laughs, the fake-vomit sounds, but instead, I hear the sounds of claps. The whole class is clapping, and they're clapping for me. It astounds me. They're not making fun of me or mocking me or calling me names, they're cheering for me.

35

It's Saturday morning. Aunty Dawn is at the kitchen table when I come out of my room with my packed duffel bag. She's got a cup of tea and she's reading the *Koori Mail* while Archie Roach's 'Mother's Heartbeat' is playing quietly on the stereo.

'Morning, Aunt,' I say. I take a seat at the table with her.

'You packed everything you need?' she asks, looking over my duffel bag.

'Yesssss,' I say. 'It's all good.'

Aunty Dawn smiles and reaches across the table to rest her hand over mine.

'You're growing into a very handsome young man,' she says. 'But you'll always be my little Jamie-baby.'

I chuckle with her as Uncle Bobby rinses his coffee cup in the sink, saying he'll drive me to the bus stop after he's had a quick shower.

'I wrote a poem at school,' I say to Aunty Dawn. I pull a folded piece of paper from my pocket and hand it to her. She unfolds it and squints her eyes.

'You know Aunty's eyes aren't too good these days,' she says. 'You'll need to read it for me, Jamie.'

I take the paper and gaze over the words I wrote. *No. Not this one.*

'I'll be back,' I say as I dart to my room. I head to the bookshelf, grab *Lemons in the Chicken Wire* and take out the poem I wrote about Aunty Dawn when I was in juvie. I head back to the kitchen and take my seat.

'This one's called "Aunty/Mum",' I say. I'm not as nervous as I was when I read the poem to Shae or when Mr Barrett read 'The Dark Place' to my English class. I'm not embarrassed by it, either. It's poetry. I want Aunty Dawn to hear it.

'Mother. Aunty.

Carer. Protector.

Watcher. Guardian...'

III

When I finish reading, Aunty Dawn stands and waddles to me, gives me a hug and a kiss.

'You're full of surprises, Jamie,' she says. 'I'm very proud of you. Thank you. That was beautiful.'

We have breakfast together before Uncle Bobby drives me to the bus stop in town. He's got his Johnny Cash CD playing on the stereo. I've got butterflies in my stomach. I haven't ever taken a bus trip on my own. Trey said he'll meet me near the stop at Central Station, but I haven't ever been to Sydney before, either.

'Fuck's sake,' Uncle Bobby mutters to himself as we turn onto the main street of Dalton's Bay. There's a line-up of four cars ahead of us, where the cops are doing breath tests. We roll up slowly and my heart begins to race when I see the officer doing the breath tests is Constable Minelli. He holds his breathalyser to Uncle Bobby's mouth and, as Uncle Bobby breathes into it, Minelli looks at me. Our eyes stick to each other's for a moment, then I look away. The breathalyser beeps.

'You're good to go,' Minelli says to Uncle Bobby. We drive away and I relax back in my seat.

'That the copper who roughed you fullas up?' Uncle Bobby asks.

I nod. 'One of them.'

We arrive at the bus stop and Uncle Bobby pulls into the drop-off zone.

'You right then?' he asks.

'Yeah, think I got everything.'

I get out and grab my duffel bag from the back and the pillow I've fixed between the carry-straps.

'Stand tall when you see them,' Uncle Bobby says. 'Show them the man you've become.'

'Yeah, I will.'

'See you when you get back on Monday.'

'Yep. See ya, Unk.'

Uncle Bobby leaves and my phone vibrates. It's a message from Dally:

Stevie's birthday party tomorrow night. You in or what?

I don't want to go back to Stevie's. I stuff my phone back into my pocket, knowing I'm not going to reply. I think about Lenny in his new life, in his new home and city. It's easy for him to leave us behind. It feels like it's already a little easier for me too.

I join the line of travellers as the bus pulls in. I'm surprised so many people are taking the bus up the coast today. I find a seat near the back and against the window. The bus has seatbelts, so I buckle myself in, sit back and look to the main street.

As we leave town over the bridge and set out along the beach, I text Trey to tell him I'm on my way. In a few hours, I'll be in Sydney. Trey will take me to his house and I'll meet his partner, Jacob. Tomorrow, I'll jump in the car with Trey and we'll go to The Entrance. There, I'll see my parents again. For Dad, it could be the last time. I don't know what I'll say to him when I see him. I imagine he will be smaller than I remember. Maybe he's got a beard. Maybe his hair will be grey. Or maybe he'll look exactly as I remember him: brown skin, brown eyes, short black hair, goatee with a few strands of grey growing in places.

I'll be back in Dalton's Bay on Monday, but as the bus veers away from the beach and speeds up to one hundred on the highway, it feels like a goodbye.

A goodbye.

Those words are rushing in again. Luckily, I packed my exercise book. I turn to a new page and write a title for my next poem: 'A Goodbye'.

When I'm done, I close my book and look out the window. The bus arrives in Kinston City for a pick-up. The town looks so beautiful outside – families are walking along the main street, carrying groceries, little kids trying to keep up. There's a pair of seagulls landing on a shop's gutter, visiting from the nearby beach. Yet this beautiful town is home to a terrible place – a place I never want to see again – and my chest feels heavy, suddenly filled with stones, knowing the juvie is near.

A lady and her child, a toddler, get on the bus. The lady is Koori and for a moment, I think she's Shae. She has the same hair as Shae, but she's not her. I wonder if I'll ever see Shae again.

36

I wake from a nap just as the bus is rolling into the city of Sydney. I double-check the instructions in Trey's last text – I take a right-hand turn after stepping off the bus and walk uphill for a bit until I get to Central Station. The sun's out, but it's pretty cold.

I spot Trey's black Toyota Corolla in the car park. He's leaning against the door finishing a cigarette, which he flicks away when he sees me approaching.

'Your bus was late,' he says.

'Sorry, I don't have any power over the bus driver,' I reply.

Trey smiles and I load my bag onto the back seat and climb into the car. As we drive out of the city, Trey sits forward with his chin pretty much kissing the steering wheel, swearing and complaining about the traffic.

'This is the absolute worst,' Trey says as we head along Parramatta Road. 'I always have visions of my death when I drive along here.'

We head onto the motorway and the traffic is phenomenal. I swear two hours have passed by the time Trey announces, 'Here we are: Werrington. Home, sweet home.'

We drive through some streets and arrive at a big white building. The paint is faded on the bricks. Trey carries my duffel bag for me as we head into the building. Inside, a white light fills the entrance corridor. There are two units on the ground floor and a lift with yellow tape across it.

'Been waiting for that to get fixed for two months at least,' Trey says as we start up the stairs to his apartment on level three.

It smells like scented candles as I follow Trey inside. The footy's on and I can hear Phil Gould's voice complaining about something as usual. A man stands up from the couch when he sees us walk into the lounge room. He's tall and looks muscly in his blue shirt. He's got brown hair and a short, well-maintained beard. And he's white. For some reason, that surprises me.

'This is my partner, Jacob,' Trey says.

'Jamie,' Jacob says, stubbie of beer in one hand, extending the other to shake mine. 'I'm so glad to finally meet ya.' He looks a little older than Trey and he's got a strong handshake.

'Nice to meet you too.'

A dog barks and rushes over to me. It's a little Maltese terrier.

'Valerie,' Trey says, crouching down. She stops barking and I crouch down too as Trey caresses her head. 'Valerie, this is my little brother, Jamie.'

I pat Valerie and she wags her tail.

'Nice to meet you, Valerie,' I say.

'Lucky for you, our roommate moved out last month, so we've got a spare room,' Trey says. He takes my bag to the spare room as I join Jacob on the couch in front of the TV. Newcastle Knights are playing Canberra Raiders, and the Raiders are winning comfortably.

I gotta admit, the building didn't really look like much from the outside, but Trey and Jacob have a pretty neat apartment. Their TV is a good size, they've got a clean, comfy couch, which looks brand new, and there is not a stray lolly wrapper or crumb or anything on the spotless floor. I'm guessing they vacuumed the place before I arrived.

Jacob heads to the kitchen and returns with two fresh Coopers pale ales. He hands one to Trey when he joins us on the couch and we all watch the footy together.

'So, what was Trey like as a kid?' Jacob asks me, as Trey orders us charcoal chicken and chips for dinner. 'I hear he was a bit of an angsty fireball.'

'Umm, I dunno. He was sort of like a third parent sometimes. He was always worried about me getting hurt or telling me not to do something. But yeah, he was always angry when he was a teenager. So, to sum it up, he was an arsehole.'

Jacob chuckles.

'He was a good big brother, though,' I say. I tell Jacob the story of when I fell off my bike and broke my leg, and how Trey carried me all the way home on his back.

After dinner, Trey heads to his room and comes out holding a pocket-sized photo album. He hands it to me and I rest back on the couch under the downlights. The first photo I see when I open the album is one of Trey as a toddler. He's just in his jocks, wearing one of those paper crowns you get out of Christmas bonbons. There's chocolate around his mouth and he's licking his lips.

'Wow, you used to be skinny,' I say to Trey. He blushes.

I turn the page and there's a photo of a baby wrapped in a white blanket, resting in someone's arms.

'That's you,' Trey says.

'No way.'

I turn the page again and there's a photo of me and Trey in front of a Christmas tree. I'm wearing Wiggles pyjamas and Trey's wearing Buzz Lightyear ones. I'm still a baby and I'm sitting in the lap of an Aboriginal woman with long black hair.

'That's us with Mum,' Trey says.

'We look like a real family,' I say. I flick the page and it's a photo of Dad holding me, flexing the little muscles on his other arm with a funny look on his face, like he's in mid-roar. My eyes are wide and I'm looking at the camera, like I'm wondering what's going on.

'Dad looks different from how he does in my head,' I say to Trey.

'Yeah?'

I flick the page to look at the next photo. 'His face. The shape just looks different from what it does in my memories.'

I get to the last photo in the book. It's me and Trey with Mum. I'm older, probably five. We're at the beach. Mum's in the middle, with her hands on mine and Trey's shoulders as we stand on either side of her. We're all smiling and the wind is messing Mum's hair. Waves are rolling behind us. I can almost feel the warm sand beneath my feet, Mum's hand on my shoulder.

'There aren't any photos of all four of us together,' I say.

'Yeah, I noticed that,' Trey says, as he takes the photo album back from me. 'I guess one of them always had to hold the camera.'

I close the door of Trey's spare room behind me after I walk in. I can't get the image out of my head: me, Trey and Mum smiling at the beach.

I pull back the sheets of the single bed and climb in. I really wish I had a photo of the four of us together in the same frame. A tear is threatening to leak from the corner of my eye. I'm suddenly wide awake and my heart begins to race a little faster, because tomorrow, I'm seeing my parents again.

37

Me and Trey hit the road at eleven a.m., onto the Pacific Highway towards the Central Coast.

'I called Mum this morning to let her know we're coming,' Trey says. We listen to his playlist on the drive, and after a few songs, 'A Child Was Born Here' by Archie Roach comes on. It makes me think of Aunty Dawn. I hope she doesn't feel like I'm betraying her or anything. She's *Mum* to me too.

Trey yawns as we arrive at The Entrance. It's late afternoon. The traffic is pretty hectic here as well. Everyone's gotta get somewhere. I begin to feel nervous as Trey's GPS announces, 'In six hundred metres, the destination is on the left.'

The street is long and busy and stacked with parked cars and apartment buildings with small courtyards between them. Trey pulls into the driveway of a tall, bricked building. It must be at least eight storeys high. My heart begins to race as we pull into the visitors' car park and Trey turns off the engine. I get out of the car. My palms are sweaty and my hands are shaking.

I follow Trey up a staircase and when we get to level two, into a hallway.

I feel like running away. My throat is dry and itchy. I need water.

I worry that I won't recognise Mum and Dad – that they won't look the way I remember them. I worry their eyes will have changed, that they might not even recognise me. I worry they will be disappointed. The kid they knew was different to the person I am now. I worry that will make them angry, that I won't be good enough for them anymore.

'You right?' Trey asks.

I nod. 'All good.'

'Here we are.'

Trey knocks on the door of number twenty. Footsteps boom on the floor inside, getting louder and closer. The chain tickles the back of the wooden door, then the knob turns.

The door opens and a woman stands there in the doorway. She's short, Aboriginal. She's got wrinkles on her face, brown hair tied in a ponytail. She smiles the widest smile and I know it's Mum standing in front of me.

'My babies,' she says. Our eyes lock and Mum steps towards me. 'Jamie.'

Her arms wrap tight around me and I can't stop the tears coming to my eyes as I hug her back. She cries too, and we stand there in the doorway. It's like I've been climbing the highest mountain for years, straining every muscle in my body to get to the top and now I'm there, crying from the relief of being in her arms again. My shoulders can rest again and I surrender to her arms.

Mum releases me, steps back and wipes the tears from her eyes. She looks over me, her hand on her cheek.

'Look how big you are. You've grown all the way up. My baby, my handsome young man.'

She steps aside and I follow Trey into the apartment. It's a small place. I head into the living room. A chair slides across the hardwood floor of the kitchen. An Aboriginal man stands from the seat. He takes a moment to straighten his back as I walk to him. He's shorter than I remember him being and I'm taller than he is. He's got greying curly hair and a bald spot on top. He's skinny and I can make out the shapes of his cheekbones, covered in a five o'clock shadow.

Dad.

'Look at you.' Dad chuckles. He places his hands on my shoulders and looks me up and down.

'He's the spittin' image of ya when you were his age, Phil,' Mum says to Dad.

'He's just missing my curly hair,' Dad says.

Time isn't measurable. It's a blur and my ears feel hot. Mum sits on the couch and I follow Trey's lead and bring over a chair from the little kitchen table.

'Do youse want a cuppa?' Dad asks. He heads to the kettle and flicks it on.

'Yeah, coffee with milk and two sugars,' Trey says.

'Jamie?' Dad asks.

'Just a glass of water, thanks.'

The kettle boils and Dad starts dishing the sugar into his and Trey's cups.

'We just got back from Alice Springs,' Dad says from the kitchen. 'We took the buses over there to see cousin Eddie. You fullas never met him. He agreed to sell us his old Ford Falcon cheap, so we went over to get it. We tried to drive back to Sydney, but the head gasket blew and we broke down about fifteen kilometres outside of Euston.'

Mum sighs. 'I warned your father it wasn't worth going all that way for a Ford.'

'Anyway,' Dad continues, clearing his throat, 'we had to walk to town and ended up sleeping in some park before we hitchhiked back to Sydney.'

'We stayed a few days with the mob in the Blue Mountains,' Mum says. She turns to me. 'All my mob live there. We never got to take you boys up for a visit, so you haven't met them yet.'

'Jamie,' Dad says, 'I heard you got into some trouble.'

'Yeah, a bit. It was a one-off though. I won't be goin' back to that place,' I say.

'Good,' Dad says. 'I had a few stints in juvie myself when I was around your age, but we called it the boys' home then. I'm sure you know I've been locked up a few times. It's no good, son. You don't want to go down that path. Believe me.'

'I know,' I say. 'The only good thing about lock-up was this worker named Shae. She was different to the screws. She talked to me. She listened to me. She taught me about poetry and I wrote a poem. She really liked it. My English teacher reckons I got *creative flair,* or whatever, so I might be all right at poetry.'

'Poetry?' Mum asks. 'I used to love reading. My favourite book was *The Hobbit*. I read it five times when I was in high school. I used to like writin' too. Maybe that's where you get that *creative flair*. You definitely don't get it from your father. He's about as creative as a plank of wood.'

Dad scoffs as he brings his and Trey's cups of coffee to the lounge. He rushes back to the kitchen and pours me a glass of water. He passes it to me and sits on the couch with Mum. They both gaze over us, smiling, eyes wide open and teary.

'Thanks for coming to see us, boys,' Dad says. 'Jamie, I know you didn't want to, and I understand that, but I'm glad you're here. It means the world to me and your mother.'

'All good,' I say.

Dad takes a deep breath, rests his arm around Mum's shoulders.

'Doc said I've got nine months, but I reckon I prolly got another year left in me,' Dad says. 'Doc reckons it was too far gone when they caught it.'

'You don't seem too depressed about it,' I say.

'Nah. It is what it is.'

'Glad you finally got a couch that doesn't smell like pissy dog hair,' Trey says.

Dad laughs and smiles.

I'm remembering something. A hot day, a long time ago. The sun was stinging and my feet were dirty and wet on the grass in the backyard. I was growing out of the board shorts I was wearing and they were tight around my waist. Trey was chasing me, spraying me with his super-soaker water gun. I was trying to get away when I caught a glimpse of Dad's face. He was standing in the doorway, looking into the backyard with a VB in his hand. He was smiling, with a younger face. His hair was blacker then, and the curls were longer, but it's still the same smile.

III

The sun is setting through the window. I go with Trey on foot to the fish and chips shop at the end of the street. It's cold out and I fold my arms as we walk to keep myself warm. Trey heads into the shop and comes out with the fish and chips wrapped in butcher's paper.

Back at the apartment, Trey unwraps the fish and chips at the table and we all sit around. The salty smell fills the room. Mum squirts some of the lemon, then she's the first to the piece of battered blue grenadier. She breaks off a small bit and I take my fingers to the fish next. It's hot to the touch, but I break off a chunk. I couple it with a few chips and shove them in my mouth. My mouth fills with saliva and I swear it's the best fish I've ever tasted. I lick the chicken salt from my fingers.

'It's so good to have you both here,' Mum says. 'You're on our minds every day. You've both grown all the way up. It's been too long since we've all been together.'

'We're here now, Mum,' Trey says.

'Yeah,' I say. 'We're here now.'

I pull out my phone, navigate to my camera. All the photos I've seen of us feel like they were taken in a different lifetime. Now that we're here, I want to save this moment.

'Can we get a photo?' I ask. 'All four of us?'

'Come on, then,' Mum says. She shuffles closer to Dad at the centre of the couch and Trey sits at the end. I hold my phone in front of me and we're all smiling on my phone's screen.

I take the photo and examine it on my phone. We look so happy, but behind my smile, I want to ask my parents why they didn't get me and Trey back. I want to ask them why they didn't stick around, why they just took off. I want to tell them how much that messed me up, how I asked Aunty Dawn for them every day until one day, I gave up. I want to ask them how they could just move on with their lives without us.

I want to be angry. I should be angry. Anger should be coming so easily to me, bursting out of my chest in the blink of an eye. But as I rest back in my chair, as I stare at my mother and my father and Trey, a smile comes to my face. They smile back at me and I'm warm. I'm all good.

A feeling is coming over me – a feeling I'm not used to. It's a feeling I've had before, but one that's been gone for so long: happiness.

If happiness was a river
I've just swung from the branch
Let go of the rope
And cannonballed into happiness –
Right in the deep of it.

The feeling is overwhelming and it's soaking all over me, from the tips of my toes to the hair on my head.

We're a family again.

Again, a family.

ACKNOWLEDGEMENTS

Let me tell you: writing this book has been a roller-coaster. Thank you so much to my publisher, Jodie Webster of Allen & Unwin, for your guidance and support. This book was a lot of work and I could never have gotten it into the shape it needed to be in without you. Thank you also to my editor, Sophie Splatt, for jumping on board with me and working so hard to get my writing looking good enough for the readers.

Thank you to Varuna the National Writers' House. I began writing this book in 2019 and after a year, I felt like I was stuck and not sure where to go or what to do with the story – there was something about it that wasn't right yet. I was awarded a Copyright Agency First Nations Fellowship to spend a week at Varuna in late 2020 and the magic of Varuna brought this book to life. Going into Varuna, I knew I had a story to tell but, at Varuna, I figured out how to say what

I wanted to say. Thank you to Veechi, Amy, Vera and Sheila for looking after me at Varuna, and Peter Minter for your support during that residency.

I need to thank my friends and family for your ongoing encouragement of my writing. Your support propelled me to get this book written. A special mention goes to my little sister, Hayleigh, who is my biggest fan and always the first to read my writing.

Thank you to my friends Gabbie Stroud and Kate Liston-Mills for your continued support. I knew I found my people when our awesome friendship began. You've championed me from the day I told you I was working on this story, encouraged me to continue when it was getting difficult and always reminded me to remember why this story needed to be told.

Thank you to my partner, Matthew, for supporting me through the edits for this book, for allowing me to spend time alone with this story and for waking me up at 2 a.m. to tell me you had finished an early draft and that you loved it.

Finally, I want to thank all those Indigenous and non-Indigenous mentors, youth workers and support workers who support First Nations children, and make no mistake, they are children, who are locked up and isolated and told they are criminals. I've had lunch with a ten-year-old boy who was half my height, wondering how the hell it was okay that he was locked up behind tall walls and barbed wire. I've had a conversation with a seventeen-year-old boy who was so institutionalised, he stated he felt safer in juvie with the strict routines and certainty of meals and a bed. As someone who has worked in supporting Aboriginal children and young people in the youth justice system and out-of-home care, I know how hard it can be to keep going when you're working within a system that is at times allergic and resistant to change and progress, when all you want to do is help. I thank you for supporting our kids and hope that you'll keep going.

Thank you to those young people I worked with between 2016 and 2021. It was my job to support and encourage you but, in turn, you inspired me more than you know. I wrote this book for you and for all those kids like Jamie whose stories are never heard.

'A lightning bolt to the soul. *The Boy from the Mish*
announces a bold, necessary new talent.'
WILL KOSTAKIS

'I loved it! Oh my god, I loved it so much. What a tender,
romantic, beautiful, hopeful, wonderful novel! Never before
have I read a book where two First Nations teenage boys
are given the chance to fall in love, cry, think of each other
as beautiful and explore their feelings and their bodies in
such an authentic and moving way. *The Boy from the Mish* is
an extraordinary debut novel. Jackson and Tomas stole my
heart, and I'll be thinking about them for a long time.'
NINA KENWOOD

'How I wish I had this big-hearted book when I was a teenager.
It would've changed my life. Let it change yours.'
BENJAMIN LAW

'It is, honestly, a book I've been searching for over my
whole career as an editor, as well as all my years as a
(queer) reader. I'm not ashamed to say that it made me cry
(repeatedly) and awed me with the power of its storytelling
and the way it articulated so well what it's like to be struck
inarticulate by some facets of your identity, while other
facets are pronouncing themselves all too clearly.'
DAVID LEVITHAN,
Scholastic US Editorial Director

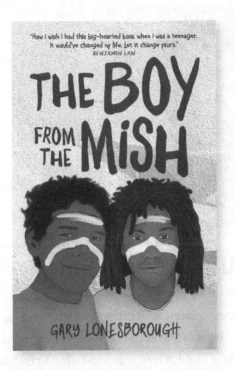

'Honest. Funny. Beautiful. This book is all the things.'
GABBIE STROUD

'*The Boy from the Mish* is a powerful and searingly honest coming-of-age novel positively brimming with heart. Gary Lonesborough has deftly woven a tale that is both a raw, unflinching look at the experience of growing up gay and Aboriginal, and a sweet, truly endearing love story you just can't turn away from. This is Own Voices storytelling at its best.'
HOLDEN SHEPPARD

ABOUT THE AUTHOR

Gary Lonesborough is a Yuin writer, who grew up on the Far South Coast of NSW as part of a large and proud Aboriginal family. As a child, Gary was a massive Kylie Minogue and North Queensland Cowboys fan who was always writing. He continued his creative journey when he moved to Sydney to study at film school. Gary has experience working in child protection, Aboriginal health, the disability sector (including experience working in the youth justice system) and the film industry, including working on the feature film adaptation of *Jasper Jones*. His debut YA novel, *The Boy from the Mish*, was published by Allen & Unwin in February 2021, and released as *Ready When You Are* in the US in 2022.